FORGOTTEN SECRETS

VANISHING RANCH, BOOK 1

CHRISTY BARRITT

PROLOGUE

JESSE MARX STARED at the four men surrounding him.

Each of them held a gun that gleamed in the midafternoon sunlight.

And Jesse was unarmed.

He would run . . . except he was on the roof of an eight-story building in Las Vegas.

With nothing but a three-foot wall stopping him from falling to the ground below.

He knew his odds in this situation.

They weren't good.

"Listen, guys, we can talk this out." He decided to rely on his intellect rather than his physical prowess right now.

He was too outnumbered to win this battle otherwise.

One of the men—Lukas—stepped closer. "Who are you working for?"

The scar across the man's cheek hinted of the fights he'd been in—the fights where he'd come out as conqueror. His dark hair was cut short, and tattoos claimed nearly every visible surface of his arms and neck.

"No one. I'm not working for anyone." Jesse tried to stop the sweat from covering his forehead, a nearly impossible task.

Lukas let out a grunt that clearly showed he didn't believe Jesse. "You better start talking. You won't like the other options if you don't."

Jesse glanced behind him, and his head swam a moment as he viewed the vast drop below.

There was a *really* good chance this wasn't going to end well.

"I would tell you if I knew anything." Jesse kept his voice light. "But I don't know what you're talking about. You've got the wrong guy."

Lukas stepped closer, waving his gun in Jesse's face. "Do you think we're stupid?"

"No, I don't think you're stupid. I just think you're mistaken." Jesse *did* think they were a *little* stupid. But he'd never say that—not if he wanted to live.

"This is your last chance to answer our questions." Lukas and his comrades stepped closer, backing Jesse up until he hit the wall.

Even with all his FBI training, this would be a very tricky situation.

"Who do you work for?" Lukas demanded again. "Last chance."

Jesse knew there was no use telling this guy again that he didn't work for anyone.

Instead, he did the next best thing.

He grabbed Lukas' arm and twisted it until the gun fell out of his grasp. The man let out a whimper. With his other hand, Jesse swung his fist until it connected with the guy's jaw.

Lukas reeled back.

As he did, Jesse dove for the man's gun. He'd need it to fight off these other thugs.

But it was too late.

One of the other men bull-rushed him, giving Lukas time to recover. The man grabbed Jesse's shirt and held him over the edge.

Jesse glanced down at the nothingness beneath him.

At once, his life flashed before his eyes.

He couldn't fail.

Not just in this situation. But with this whole assignment.

He'd come too far. Sacrificed too much.

He glanced back at Lukas. "Can't we talk this through?"

"We're beyond talking." Lukas glared at him before letting go.

Jesse flailed as he felt nothing but air beneath him.

CHAPTER
ONE

JESSE MARX FELT his world spinning.

He was in danger.

He had to do something.

Had to stop this.

But it was already too late . . .

As something tickled his face, he abruptly jerked from a deep sleep.

He rushed to his feet, his hands fisted and ready to fight. He ignored the pain in his side and the pounding in his head as adrenaline surged through him.

A hideous monster stared at him from above.

Jesse blinked.

No, not a hideous monster.

A horse.

A very curious horse.

He took a step back and hit the rough wooden wall behind him. As a wave of dizziness washed over him, he collapsed into some hay.

The scent of manure and sweaty horses floated around him, and flies buzzed in his ears.

Was he in a stable?

How in the world had he gotten here?

He touched his temple and tried to recall his last memories.

But it was almost as if a blank spot existed in his mind.

The last thing Jesse remembered was being confronted by the cartel on a rooftop.

Being held over a wall.

And beginning the fall to his death.

After that, there was . . . nothing.

He should be dead right now.

Was he losing his mind?

His heart raced harder.

As an FBI agent who'd done one too many undercover assignments, Jesse couldn't risk letting his guard down. That's why none of this made sense.

Based on the dry air around him and the sandy ground, he guessed he was in a desert climate.

Mexico maybe? Had the Campeche Cartel taken him somewhere?

The cartel was one of the most dangerous in the

United States and Mexico. Jesse had been undercover with them for the past year. He'd been feeding info to his FBI handler in hopes of taking the entire organization down.

But he'd been made.

Someone had figured out who he really was, and now the entire cartel wanted him to pay.

Or had he imagined the entire roof episode?

No, he hadn't.

Maybe they'd saved him, only to bring him here and toy with him.

Jesse had no idea.

But he had to get out of here.

First, he had to get past this horse staring him down.

Just as Jesse pulled himself back to his feet, he noticed a woman watching him. Her arms were casually draped on the edge of the horse stall. Her intelligent eyes studied him, an equal mix of amusement and caution.

Jesse stared at her a moment. At the wavy, sunkissed blonde hair that came to her shoulders. Her even features. Her slim arms.

"You might want to stay put," she said with a heavy Southern drawl. "You move around too much, and you could fall and hit your head again. That wouldn't be good."

Jesse stiffened. He'd never seen this woman before, and she acted entirely too familiar with him for his liking.

"Move the horse out of my way," he ordered.

"Sorry. Can't do that. You're here to stay for a while—like it or not."

He bristled as his survival instincts kicked in again. This woman was keeping him here against his will—and she was talking crazy.

He started to step forward.

But his head swam.

He paused to steady himself.

Instead, he scowled at the woman in front of him. She didn't look like a criminal, but that didn't mean she wasn't. "I'm an FBI agent, and you're in serious trouble. When backup finds me, you'll be facing felony charges for abduction—among other things."

"I'm not too concerned." She shrugged, seemingly unaffected.

"Who are you?" He fisted his hands, not liking the uncertainty he felt.

The woman tilted her head, her eyes glimmering. "You really don't remember?"

"I really don't." His voice came out as a growl.

"I'm Sienna . . . your wife."

Sienna Fleming stared at Jesse, trying to erase any trace of amusement from her gaze. This was not the time for her off-beat sense of humor to show itself.

But still . . . seeing tough guy Jesse Marx looking so disheveled brought her a certain amount of pleasure.

He let out a laugh before quickly shaking his head in disbelief. Sienna saw the thoughts washing over him in waves.

Doubt.

Uncertainty.

Confusion.

Then total and complete denial.

"I'm not married," he finally announced.

She shrugged. "I'm sorry to tell you, but you are."

At her words, he glanced at his left hand. His eyes widened when he saw the gold band on his ring finger.

Sienna hid her smile at his shock.

"You don't understand. I vowed to *never* get married. *And* I've never seen you before. Unless you drugged me." He narrowed his eyes. "Did you drug me and make me marry you?"

Sienna let out a laugh this time. "Don't flatter yourself, cowboy."

"Cowboy?" He raked a hand through his hair. "You need to start explaining what's going on here.

And if I'm your husband—which I'm not—why am I waking up in a horse stall?"

"Slow down. It's a long story."

"I've got time." He narrowed his eyes. "Apparently, I'm a captive audience."

"A little dramatic, don't you think? Anyway, let's go inside. I'll explain everything there."

"An explanation sounds great."

As Jesse took a step forward, he nearly stumbled. He reached for his abdomen and lifted his T-shirt to reveal a long row of stitches there. Twenty altogether.

He stared at the sutures in surprise. "What . . . ?"

"You really do need to be careful." Sienna had tried to warn him, but he hadn't listened.

He narrowed his eyes again as he glared at her. "Did you do this to me? Harvest my organs or something? Is this some kind of sick game?"

Suddenly, all the humor left Sienna. This really *wasn't* an amusing situation. In some circumstances, maybe. But not with so much on the line.

Her fun was over, and now she needed to get down to business.

"Come on." She nodded toward the door beside her. "Let's get you inside and get you something to drink. Then you're going to want to meet Charlie."

"Charlie?"

"It will all make sense soon enough." Sienna paused before adding, "I hope."

"You hope?" He stared at her again as if she'd lost her mind.

"The whole situation is complicated, to say the least."

Sienna had known the time would come when Jesse would come out of his stupor, and she'd have to explain everything. She hadn't been sure how he would react to all that had happened since his rescue.

But now she prayed she'd have the wisdom to say the right words.

She had to convince Jesse to stay and help her.

She had no other choice.

And Jesse had no other choice either . . . except he didn't know it yet.

Three people were already dead, and he was their best chance at finding answers.

Sienna opened the door to the stall, gave Winnie's nose a gentle rub, and then started toward Jesse.

The man was handsome, but in a rebellious way. He had cool, assessing brown eyes. Don't-care hair. And he *loved* that black leather jacket of his.

Only that had been removed at the hospital and sent home with him in a flimsy plastic bag.

Even without the jacket, he still gave off the same tough guy vibes.

He tried to take another step forward on his own, but he nearly keeled over with pain.

"Let me help you." She inched toward him. "It's the least I can do . . . husband dearest. That has a nice ring to it, doesn't it? I mean if I were a sixties housewife or something."

Sixties housewife was about as far from how anyone would describe Sienna as the Grand Canyon was from the Sahara Desert.

Jesse narrowed his eyes at her again. Honestly, Sienna couldn't blame him.

No doubt the situation seemed overwhelming.

But when Jesse heard the truth, he would *really* feel overwhelmed.

As would anyone in his shoes.

CHAPTER TWO

DESPITE HIS INJURIES, Jesse's muscles were bristled as he prepared himself for whatever might come next. Sienna led him from the stable, and he soaked in his surroundings. He needed to retain every detail possible if he wanted to escape this situation with his life.

The dusty ground had the small, scattered vegetation typical for a desert climate. Eight buildings dotted the landscape, all designed in a Spanish revival style. A fence with an iron gate appeared to surround the property, and the land beyond the fence stretched on for miles and miles, only to stop at imposing purple mountains that rose in the distance.

Sienna led him inside a large, stucco-sided building. A sign reading Mess Hall hung over a door on one side. She took him through another door where a small lobby waited, lined by four offices on the sides.

"Right over here," she murmured.

She led him into an office.

A thick, muscular man with short hair stood behind a desk across from him, making no secret that he was studying Jesse. Sienna leaned against the doorframe as if daring him to try to escape.

Jesse would hear what this guy had to say, and then he'd figure out his next plan of action. His injuries wouldn't allow him the prowess he desired, despite the adrenaline pumping through him. But he was prepared to fight if it came down to it.

"Charlie can't be here. There was an emergency." The man crossed his thick arms over his chest. "I'll be taking over in the meantime."

"Who are you?" Jesse demanded as he eyed the man.

"Monroe, Charlie's right-hand man. I'm sorry to have to introduce myself to you this way."

He stared at the man but said nothing. For some reason, the guy looked vaguely familiar—though Jesse couldn't remember why. He'd figure that out later.

"Why don't you both have a seat so we can all talk?" Monroe nodded to the empty seats in front of him.

Jesse obliged—for now.

He didn't like things being out of his control.

During his years undercover, control had been essential at all times lest he give himself away and blow his operation.

Feeling vulnerable and exposed wasn't something he was used to.

But he'd somehow messed up, hadn't he? He must have. He'd been made by the cartel, and they'd confronted him.

Were these two somehow associated with the men who'd cornered him on the roof?

Possibly.

His guard rose even higher.

"I'm sure you have a lot of questions." Monroe lowered himself behind the desk and steepled his hands in front of him. "We'll try to address all of them for you. Why don't we start at the beginning?"

Jesse stared at Monroe a moment before demanding, "Where am I?"

"Arizona."

"Arizona?" He'd guessed Mexico, but he wasn't that far off. "How did I get here?"

"It all started when you fell off a roof almost a week ago," Sienna told him.

Jesse's eyes widened. "Almost a week? You've got to be kidding?"

She shook her head. "Unfortunately, I'm not. You were very touch-and-go there for a while."

He rubbed his temples, wishing he could flip a switch and regain his memories. "The last thing I remember was falling. There was nothing below to catch me. How did I even survive?"

Sienna and Monroe exchanged a glance, and Jesse braced himself for whatever they were about to say.

Did these people work for the cartel he'd been undercover with?

And if they weren't the cartel . . . what if they were an even more formidable foe?

Jesse was going to have to think quick on his feet if he wanted to get through this.

Sienna drew in a deep breath, knowing this wouldn't be a fun conversation. But she was prepared for it. In all her years working for the state department, she'd learned to put up walls. If she hadn't, she would have been an emotional wreck.

But perhaps she *was* an emotional wreck, just in a different way—a way that meant that nothing ever affected her.

Not even getting married to a man she didn't know.

"So, what happened to me after I fell off the roof?" Impatience tinged Jesse's voice.

"The timing was uncanny. Just a few seconds difference, and you would have been roadkill." Monroe shrugged as if talking about something mundane.

That was Monroe for you. He was as solid as a rock—physically and emotionally. Unflappable. Dependable. Protective.

Jesse waited for them to continue.

"You're not even going to believe what I have to say," Sienna continued. "*I* almost can't believe it. The whole thing was like something from a movie. We saw you falling and knew we couldn't get to you in time. But a dump truck pulled up just at the right moment, and you landed inside. Some trash broke your fall."

Jesse raised an eyebrow, appearing as if they were trying to pull one over on him. "Really?"

She shrugged. "I told you that you weren't going to believe it."

"And then?" He still didn't sound fully convinced that she was telling the truth.

"We were able to retrieve you," Sienna said. "But you were in pretty bad condition. Even after we made sure you had the medical attention you needed, we weren't certain you were going to make it."

"And somehow this led to you marrying me?"

Sienna and Monroe exchanged another glance. This was where their story got tricky.

"We couldn't let you stay in the hospital," she said. "It wasn't safe—especially since we knew those people on the roof were determined to kill you."

"The Campeche Cartel, you mean?" His gaze darkened as he clearly read between the lines.

"Yes, we spotted several members lingering near the hospital and knew they would come for you. Hospital staff didn't want to release you, so we had to get creative."

"Did you think about calling the FBI?"

Sienna ignored his question. "Monroe and I both have some medical training so we knew we could take care of you. But we had to get you out of the hospital first, which was complicated. We couldn't make any type of medical decisions for you since we were strangers. So, we did what we had to do."

"You forged a marriage certificate?"

Sienna let out a scoffing laugh. "No, that wouldn't be very ethical."

"But marrying me when I'm unconscious is?" His voice rose in pitch.

"You weren't *unconscious*. Slightly sedated maybe.

But that's beside the point. I don't know what to say except that it was a necessary evil. I needed medical power of attorney over you so I could get you out of the hospital."

"And you couldn't just tell them we were married? You couldn't just sneak me out of the hospital when no one was looking?"

"If only it were that simple." She shrugged. "Thankfully, I have a few connections. My friend made sure all the proper legal papers were in place. She even added a few photos of us together on social media, just to make our relationship look real. She's *very* talented."

His dark mood only continued to darken. "There was no other way you could get me to a safe place— if this truly is a safe place? I mean, why did I wake up in a stable?"

"When you started coming around, you were obstinate—as to be expected," Monroe said. "You began to lash out, and we had to give you a sedative. We decided it was safer to leave you in the horse stall until you—"

"Stabilized." Sienna shrugged. "Get it? *Stable*-ized? Too soon to make that joke?"

Monroe gave her a look.

Her smile slipped. "Anyway, we did put out fresh, clean hay for you. In case you were wondering."

"How thoughtful." Jesse touched his temple and winced when he felt the knot there. His head pounded harder at the realization. "And my memories? Why has almost an entire week disappeared?"

"Like I said, you had a bad head injury. Trauma like that can cause lapses in memory. Your memories will resurface sometime . . . probably."

"This seems over the top," he said. "*You* seem over the top."

She shrugged. "I don't make it a habit of marrying strangers, if that's what you're suggesting."

"So, are you saying I'm your first hostage husband?"

"I'm saying if I didn't marry you and get you out of there, the cartel would have found you and killed you."

Her words hung in the air.

But she also needed to tell him that she and Monroe had singled him out for a reason.

They needed his help. Now they needed to convince him to trust them.

CHAPTER
THREE

GET TO A COMPUTER. *Steal a phone. Find a weapon.*

The list replayed in Jesse's mind. Doing those things were his best hope of escaping.

In normal circumstances, he would fight. But not with his current injuries.

Besides, Monroe had a gun holstered at his shoulder. Plus, the guy was big. Football player big and brawny.

Jesse was in danger right now. He was certain of it.

He just couldn't figure out who these guys worked for.

None of the words leaving Sienna's mouth made sense. If these two knew he was in danger, why didn't they just call the police?

Jesse still had so many more questions, but his thoughts felt fuzzy. Even his rushing adrenaline didn't seem to help him clear his mind. He just needed to play it cool—for now.

But for some reason, these two seemed to want him alive. If they'd wanted to kill him, Jesse would already be dead.

"What am I doing here?" Jesse asked. "What am I *really* doing here? You didn't go through all that trouble simply to save me from the cartel."

Monroe's gaze locked with his. "You're right. We need your help."

"Who is *we*?"

"Me. Charlie. Sienna."

"So, let me get this straight. You rescued me, forced me into marriage, had me discharged from the hospital, brought me to this place in the middle of nowhere, and now you want my help?" Jesse couldn't keep the tinge of bitterness out of his voice.

Monroe's gaze remained unwavering. "That about sums it up."

Jesse ran a hand through his hair, feeling as if he was living out a nightmare. "You're out of your mind. You're going to get into serious trouble for this. Abducting an FBI agent is a federal crime."

"Maybe we will." Monroe shrugged. "But we're twenty miles from our nearest neighbors out here—if you don't include the occasional vagrant wandering the desert. You don't have transportation, a phone, or a weapon. So, it looks like you have no choice but to hear us out."

That much was becoming obvious, and he didn't like it.

He scowled. "Even if I were in a position where I wanted to help, I'm not in a *position* to help . . . if you catch my drift."

Monroe's jaw twitched. "You made the cartel very, very angry. Snitches don't get stitches with them—snitches get bullets to the heart."

Monroe's words reminded him of the gravity of this situation.

He was injured. Had lost his memory. And he was twenty miles from the nearest neighbor.

If these two were telling the truth, Jesse was a long way from any kind of help.

He could still try to get his hands on a phone or a computer.

But his best option right now might be running.

Twenty miles was doable. He would just need to plan accordingly.

At the first opportunity, Jesse was going to flee.

He had no other choice if he wanted to survive.

But right now, he needed to hear the rest of their explanation. He'd take mental notes as he listened, knowing that any detail might be one that helped save his life.

Sienna watched Jesse's gaze harden and knew she needed to speed up this conversation. "Let me get to the point. We need your help finding a killer."

Jesse stared at her. "Why my help?"

"Because you have the connections we need. Three people have recently been killed—people associated with a military operation that took place fifteen years ago. We need to know why."

"Fifteen years ago? Was I involved in this operation?"

"No," Sienna said. "But we also need someone with your skillset, and, as an undercover agent for the FBI, you have what we're looking for."

"Back up a little. You mentioned I have connections?" Jesse asked. "Does this tie in with one of my past cases or something?"

Monroe leaned forward. "We believe you know some people involved. That's all we can say right now—until we know we have your full cooperation."

"Doesn't this seem over-the-top?" Jesse stared at them both as if waiting for one of them to crack. "Is this some type of hidden camera show? Because, if it is, it's extreme."

Sienna sobered. "This is no joke. As we were trying to figure out who might be able to help us, we began tracking you. We have reason to believe someone in the FBI blew your cover."

"What?" Jesse's voice climbed in pitch.

"We believe another agent sold you out, and that's how the cartel knew you were double-crossing them."

"No one at the FBI would do that . . ." Jesse swung his head back and forth in denial.

"For the right amount of money, someone would." Monroe shrugged, his statement matter of fact.

Jesse's eyes flickered back and forth between them, suspicion in his gaze. "How would you find that out even?"

Sienna didn't blame him for his reaction. She'd be the same way in his shoes. But she needed to proceed cautiously.

"We have our ways," she finally said. "We knew we needed to talk to you, so we did our research."

His eyes remained hard and unyielding. "I don't know if that's true or not, but let's say it is. I'm still not sure how I'm supposed to help."

"You'll need a couple of days to get stronger, of

course, and to familiarize yourself with this mission," Sienna told him. "Then we need you to help us find this killer and track down the answers we need."

His jaw hardened, and he remained quiet a moment until finally asking, "Is there any reason you guys just didn't ask me to help with this instead of kidnapping me?"

"As we said earlier, you weren't safe in the hospital. Besides, we figured you would say no." Monroe leaned back in his seat. "You saying no wasn't really an option—not when people's lives are on the line."

"This is a federal crime," Jesse reminded them again.

"We know," Sienna said. "And we regret that our methods weren't exactly savory."

"Weren't exactly savory?" He opened his mouth as if to say more but then shut it again. "For the record, I don't like being strongarmed into doing anything."

Sienna and Monroe both remained quiet, waiting for him to continue.

Finally, he asked, "When do I get to meet your boss? Charlie, you said? I need more details. This is all pretty vague right now."

"Soon." Monroe rolled his shoulders back before straightening some papers on his desk. "But I can't promise you a specific time. For now, you should go take a shower and get some rest. You've been through a lot, and your body still needs to heal."

"I've been through so much that I've apparently lost a week of my life." The dry tone of Jesse's voice and the hard set of his jaw showed his obvious irritation.

"Hopefully, that's temporary." Sienna meant the words. Losing that much time had to feel unnerving. "Some of those details might eventually return to you. You might even remember our little bedside wedding."

Jesse stared at her.

Was he repulsed at the thought of being married to her?

Sienna wasn't sure. She'd like to say that it didn't matter. She knew she was attractive. Enough people had told her that.

But for some reason, his clear rejection stirred something in her.

Instead, he said, "This marriage isn't real."

"I'm afraid it is."

Jesse continued to stare at her, still looking dumb-founded. "Why in heaven's name would you marry me?"

"Because I didn't want you to die."

He let out an exasperated sigh. "I can't even think about this anymore."

He rushed to his feet but paused as if a wave of dizziness washed over him. Once it passed, he looked back at her.

"Can you show me where I'll be staying?" he asked. "I'd like to get settled in. That shower is sounding awfully good right now."

Sienna nodded. "Of course. Right this way."

But Sienna wasn't fooled. Jesse was far from settling in.

She couldn't blame him. In fact, she looked forward to finding out just what the man was capable of.

CHAPTER
FOUR

ONCE JESSE WAS TUCKED AWAY in the bunkhouse and under the watchful eye of Hudson, one of the ranch hands, Sienna wandered back toward the mess hall. Monroe stood outside, his gaze on the bunkhouse.

"That went well." She stood beside him, also facing the bunkhouse.

Monroe, a man of few words, grunted. "Did it?"

"I thought so."

"He's lived his life undercover for most of the past decade. He very well could pretend to be on our side and backstab us."

Sienna pressed her lips together as she considered his words. "Oh, he has a plan. But I don't think backstabbing us is what he's going for."

Monroe only stared at her. "And you know this how?"

She shrugged. "It's just a gut feeling."

"A gut feeling about your new husband." He scowled before crossing his massive arms across his chest. "I told you this was a bad idea."

"We had no other choice. I've got to get Jesse on board, and I have to make sure that he trusts us."

"You have your job cut out for you."

"Yes, I do. Yes, I do." She let out a long breath that blew her bangs away from her face.

Sienna had been in some risky situations before. She'd almost lost her life uncountable times. Had been betrayed by assets. Had nearly been caught obtaining top-secret information.

But something about the stubborn determination she saw in Jesse's gaze made this situation somehow seem even more risky.

Even though the original crime they were looking into had taken place more than a decade ago, the killer responsible must have gotten spooked recently. Now, there were more dead bodies.

Someone was killing off everyone who might have any answers.

They had to stop him.

Monroe raised an eyebrow before asking, "Do you think he's going to stay?"

"Absolutely not," Sienna said. "He's looking for any opportunity he can to run—just like any self-respecting FBI agent would."

"You think he'll take a horse?"

She shook her head. "No, he didn't look comfortable around horses. Plus, he can't get out the gate with one. I think he knows that."

Monroe frowned as he glanced out the window. "He won't survive out there in the desert on foot. It's too hot. The walk is too long. He's too injured."

She nodded. "I know."

"So, what are you going to do?"

Sienna let out a long breath. She'd thought about this at length. This was something she couldn't leave to chance. "I'll follow him. But I'll let him get a distance down the road so he can think he's doing well. Maybe it'll tire him out a little. Then I'll ride up when he's at his lowest, and he'll have no choice but to come back with me."

Monroe cast her a skeptical glance. "You really think that's going to work? Jesse seems like a pretty stubborn guy."

"I'm a pretty stubborn woman."

He shifted in his chair. "You've really gone above and beyond for this assignment."

Sienna frowned and glanced at the wedding ring

on her finger. "I have. But I don't have any other choice. We need answers."

"And you're going to keep going with this whole marriage thing?"

She shrugged as she looked at the wedding ring again. "It's not a big deal."

"Marriage is *always* a big deal."

"It's just a legally binding contract."

"Or a covenant before God."

Or *that*. "Either way, I'm not concerned. All I want is justice right now."

That driving need for justice always remained at the forefront of Sienna's mind.

Maybe it wasn't completely healthy. Maybe she was a little obsessed.

But she couldn't seem to back down, no matter how hard she tried.

She let out a sigh. "I guess I better get ready for the rest of the day. It should be interesting."

Monroe straightened as if preparing himself to get back to work. "I'll be here. Just radio me if you need any backup."

"I will. But I should be fine." She crossed her arms. She would make sure of it.

Jesse let the water pound his skin.

Taking a shower had never felt so good.

If only he could let down his guard enough to enjoy it. But that wasn't even a remote possibility. Not considering everything that had happened.

This all felt like a bad dream he'd awaken from at any minute.

But he knew it wasn't.

The bunkhouse had five rooms. On the far right were the ladies' quarters with an attached bath. On the far left were the men's. In between was a common room with a small kitchenette, two couches, a TV, and a few chairs.

That's the area where a man who'd been introduced as Hudson sat, quietly reading a book while no doubt keeping an eye on Jesse.

As Jesse turned the water off, he glanced at the stitches on his abdomen. That was quite the cut he'd gotten. Then there was the bruising around it, several smaller cuts on his chest, cracked ribs, and a knot on his head.

But things could have been worse. Much worse.

As he stepped from the shower and dried off, he glanced through a high window outside.

The sun was already sinking in the distance. As soon as he knew that Sienna and Monroe were otherwise occupied, he'd make his escape.

He'd already plotted what he'd do.

Jesse would need to nourish himself before he set out. He hadn't been able to bring himself to eat the sandwich Sienna had made for him. There was a small basket sitting atop the kitchenette that had some beef jerky, dried fruit, and trail mix in it. He'd snack on those items if dinner turned out anything like the banana sandwich Sienna had fixed for him.

He'd also need to take some water with him—lots of water, especially since it was May, and temperatures outside were already hot. He'd hoped some water was stocked inside the mini-fridge he'd seen.

With the towel around his waist, he left the bathroom. Hudson still sat on the couch reading—even though Jesse knew he wasn't concentrating on his book nearly as hard as he pretended to be.

He walked to his bed and saw some clothes had been laid out for him.

Not his normal attire by any means.

Instead, he'd been left jeans, a plaid shirt, and cowboy boots.

He let out an airy laugh.

How appropriate for this ranch.

He preferred his leather jacket and low-slung jeans.

But beggars couldn't be choosers. He'd have to make this work.

He dressed and glanced at himself in the mirror, nearly blanching at his reflection.

He didn't even look like himself.

Then again, he should be used to not looking like himself. All these years undercover, Jesse had nearly lost who he really was. The line between the real Jesse and who he pretended to be seemed to be a big blur.

Sometimes, the thought left him unsettled. Made him wonder about his future. Made him question his decisions.

But those things were all water under the bridge. He'd been about to tell his boss that he wanted out. That he couldn't do any more undercover assignments.

Then he'd caught wind that the cartel was onto him. Before he could escape, they'd cornered him on that roof. He'd fallen over the edge.

But now this . . .

He glanced at his watch.

Right on cue, his prison guard—or wife— knocked on the door.

It was time for dinner.

CHAPTER FIVE

JESSE DIDN'T LIKE the amusement in Sienna's eyes as she observed him outside the bunkhouse.

"That's a nice look on you," she murmured.

"This isn't my kind of outfit." He scowled as he glanced down.

He usually didn't scowl this much. But, considering the situation, it seemed natural.

Sienna grinned at him. "Sure, it is, cowboy."

He scowled again. "I'm not a cowboy."

"If you say so." She shrugged before turning to continue walking.

Jesse grabbed her arm, hating the evasive dance they'd been engaged in since he woke in that horse stall. He had questions, and he wanted answers. She was acting as if this was a game.

"Are you out of your mind?" he asked. "For real.

You're acting like this . . . this . . . *situation* . . . is normal. Or as if it's a joke. I'm not comfortable with either."

Sienna's smile slipped. "This isn't a joke."

"Then why are you acting as if it is?"

Her gaze turned serious. "I'm just doing my job."

"You're more than doing your job. You're amused, at my expense. Besides, people don't marry other people as part of their job."

Her gaze locked with his, challenge in her eyes. "You don't worry about me. I'd say you have enough to worry about of your own, cowboy."

His eyes narrowed even more.

She *loved* calling him that, didn't she? He knew what she was really trying to do—to deflect any attention from herself.

Everything about this situation seemed wrong. So wrong. Even if they were telling the truth about these three dead people, this wasn't the way to go about solving the crime.

Jesse had to figure out a way to alert authorities about where he was. His colleagues at the FBI would send help.

Unless Sienna was right and someone at the FBI had sold him out.

But that couldn't be true.

He had a good relationship with his colleagues.

No one he worked with would do that to him.

Which still left contacting the FBI as his best choice.

"Come on." Sienna nodded toward a path in the distance. "I'll give you a quick tour of Vanishing Ranch before dinner."

Jesse wasn't interested in a tour. But he needed to figure out the lay of this place—especially if he was going to escape.

Sienna strolled beside him, looking at ease in this setting. "Aside from the bunkhouse and the mess hall, we have a recreation building, several offices, and a swimming pool."

He'd play along—for now. "Interesting. Why a swimming pool?"

"The place used to be a dude ranch where vacationers came. That closed down about eight years ago. That's when Charlie bought it."

"Good to know."

Sienna continued, "We also have eight cabanas that special guests as well as the management of this place uses. That's not you or me, so don't get your hopes up. We won't get that luxury."

"Exactly how many people work here in *the management*?" *The management* sounded like a good name for a secret underground organization that was up to no good, didn't it?

"Management? That would be Charlie, Monroe, and Chef Dean. Then we have everyone else—and everyone else includes our housekeeper, Kota, and several ranch hands."

"Sounds like quite the operation you guys have set up here." This place had to be a cover. And these people . . . did they work for the Campeche Cartel? Jesse could easily see this place being used for money laundering or some kind of trafficking detail.

It was the only thing that made sense. Because some cartels were more clever than others. They hid what they were doing behind other businesses. They had people with respectable façades as their spokesmen and women.

That was why Jesse really needed to be on guard.

He couldn't trust anyone here.

Jesse needed to keep that reminder in the back of his mind at all times even when Sienna flashed that sweet but mischievous smile at him.

Sienna sensed that Jesse wasn't warming up to being here yet. She hated that he felt so confused and uncomfortable, but she hoped with time that he'd come to understand the situation better.

She paused at the stable and let him look inside.

In the distance, Hudson brushed one of the horses. The man looked unassuming, but he was a former Navy SEAL who'd just started working here two months ago. He knew how to keep a low profile, and, thanks to growing up on a Montana ranch, he was an expert horseman.

"We take in all kinds of horses." Sienna leaned against the open stable door. "They're mostly from bad situations, and we nurse them back to health. It's really quite amazing."

Jesse stared at her as if trying to decide if she was being sincere or not. No doubt, he thought that she and Monroe were evil. He probably even wondered why evil people would want to help horses.

"The FBI has to be looking for me right now." Jesse's mind was still clearly on his sudden and unexpected arrival here.

"Honestly, they probably aren't."

He bristled, his hands going to his hips. "Why is that?"

"I told them you and I were on our honeymoon. In the Caribbean. For three weeks. Don't worry—you had that much vacation time saved up. I worked it all out for you."

Jesse bristled even more. "What? When did you talk to them?"

Sienna waved her hand in the air as if talking

about what she ate for lunch—not rearranging the course of his life. She'd learned the hard way not to make a big deal of things. It only got everyone's emotions heightened.

"As soon as we got married, I talked to ASAC Jones via Facetime," she said. "I knew we had to make an appearance together, so we did."

"When I was out of it?"

"Yes, now that you mention it. You didn't say much. You were kind of just . . . there."

"And my boss didn't notice?" Jesse asked.

"Not that he said. I gave him the news so he was focused on me."

"You told him we were married?"

"I thought we'd already been through this? There's no need to make this weird."

Jesse ran a hand through his hair in that exasperated way he kept doing. "This is already weird."

Sienna shrugged, determined not to let him see any doubt in her. She had to stay strong if she was going to make this work. "Speak for yourself."

She turned and continued walking toward the mess hall. Jesse quickly fell into step beside her.

"Did I know you before this?" he asked.

"Nope."

"And after we got married, before I lost my memories again . . . did I like you?"

His question sent a surge of amusement through her. She paused and turned toward him, placing her hands on her hips as she glanced into his question-filled gaze.

"No, you were pretty much just like this." She reached up and patted his cheek. "But that's okay. I'm very patient."

Then she turned on her heel and continued walking, the scent of smoked brisket leading the way.

"You're out of your mind. You know that, don't you?"

Sienna knew by Jesse's tone that he hadn't moved. He was planted in place right now, probably flabbergasted still.

"I'm not out of my mind," she called over her shoulder. "Just call it for what it is. I'm downright crazy. And you're along for the ride, you lucky thing."

She hadn't realized how much she'd enjoy getting under Jesse's skin.

But it was fun. Almost too fun.

Sienna smiled a moment, but it quickly faded.

The fun wouldn't last long. Jesse would make his move soon. Then they'd need to get down to some serious business.

———

Jesse tried not to show his disappointment when dinner was served, and it was a brisket sandwich and fries.

His disappointment wasn't because of the food itself. The meal looked and smelled great—plus, he was hungry.

But he'd been hoping for some utensils. He'd planned on grabbing a knife or even a fork to use as a weapon.

These guys seemed smart, like the types who might have known his plans and asked for this meal because of it.

Should he pretend to be compliant? Or should he continue to put up a fight?

He was a master at pretending to be someone he wasn't. So, if he needed to act as if he was on their side and doing what they wanted, then that was what he'd do.

Jesse wasn't sure yet. He needed more time to figure these people out first.

Then he would run.

"So, this is just a ranch?" Jesse started as he glanced around. "I don't even know how you can sustain yourself enough to pay your bills out here. Taking in horses no one else wants? That's a money pit. The land is too dry for farming. I'm guessing that the internet isn't great out here, which eliminates teleworking. That leaves me wondering exactly how you guys support yourselves."

"Easy." Sienna popped a fry in her mouth. "We bought the property outright so there's no mortgage. We get our energy from solar power, and we have our water delivered weekly. There's not a lot of overhead costs around here. That lets us do what we want without people asking a lot of questions."

Jesse's mood only darkened. He wasn't dealing with amateurs here. And this location . . . it was the perfect place to hold someone captive.

This wasn't the kind of place people just happened to come across. If Jesse had to guess, the ranch was totally off the grid. GPS probably didn't even have it on record.

He took another bite of his sandwich, surprisingly hungry and the food surprisingly good.

But he wouldn't tell Sienna or Monroe that.

Instead, his mind continued to race.

For now, he'd go along with things.

Tonight, after everyone was asleep, he'd leave.

He wasn't sure what he might face while escaping.

But he knew no matter what happened the risk was worth it.

CHAPTER
SIX

JESSE LAY in bed pretending to sleep just in case anyone checked on him. Sure enough, at eleven o'clock, Sienna stuck her head in the doorway as if to make sure he was there.

He made sure to keep his breathing even and controlled.

He'd already packed a small backpack he'd found in a closet. He added enough bottled water and plenty of snack food to get him through—he hoped.

He'd foregone taking his pain medicine—Sienna had given him exactly one pill just in case he needed it. Even though his ribs ached, he'd rather be alert and push through the pain than to take the meds and feel he wasn't at his sharpest mentally.

At 12:30, he rose.

Hudson and a couple of other ranch hands were

also staying in the bunkhouse, but they all seemed dead asleep after a hard day's work.

He pulled on his cowboy boots, wishing he had his tactical boots.

Sienna must have taken those, so these would have to work.

Quietly, he slipped the backpack over his shoulder before stepping into the main living area that separated the two sleeping areas.

All was quiet.

Part of him had expected to see Sienna sitting on the couch just waiting for him to do something.

But she wasn't there.

The thought was strange, but part of him was disappointed that he wouldn't have the time to figure her out. Certainly, there was more to her story. He wanted to know what it was.

But he didn't want to know bad enough to stick around.

The best time he could escape was at night when the sun was hidden. During the day, the temperature climbed as high as a hundred—if not higher.

Plus, he was less likely to be seen in the darkness.

Quietly, he opened the door and slipped outside.

The temperature had probably dropped into the high seventies. A breeze crept through his shirt, making it feel cooler.

But he wasn't concerned about the chill in the air.

Instead, he glanced around one more time.

He didn't see anyone.

Quietly, he began walking down the lane toward the gate in the distance.

He'd thought about taking a horse with him, but he'd never been a horse kind of guy. Plus, according to Sienna, these animals were injured in some way. The last thing he needed to do was to hop on a physically or mentally unwell horse.

He'd also thought about taking one of the vehicles he'd seen parked behind the mess hall. But by the time he hotwired one and got through the gates, everyone here would be awake.

No, he'd be better off on his own two feet.

He reached the gate. Most likely, an alarm was triggered whenever this gate opened. Instead of risking it, he hoisted his bag over the fence before climbing it and dropping to the other side.

Then he stared out at the vast nothingness around him.

Occasionally, he spotted a Joshua tree. But other than that, the terrain was just flat with yucca bushes and some other stubby desert foliage he couldn't identify.

He wasn't sure which direction the closest town

was. He only knew Monroe had said it was far away —at least twenty miles.

With that thought in mind, Jesse started toward the mountain range in the distance.

He knew leaving the ranch was risky.

But he had no other choice.

He couldn't do what these people had asked of him. He couldn't move forward not knowing whose side these people were on.

So, instead, he would escape.

Then he'd call his colleagues at the FBI and come back with reinforcements to arrest these lunatics.

He glanced at the ring on his finger.

His *wife* wasn't going to be exempt either.

"Jesse just left," Hudson texted her.

Sienna rose from her bed, already dressed.

She'd been anticipating this moment.

Jesse needed to realize just how dangerous the terrain was outside this ranch. It would knock some sense into him. Then maybe he'd be willing to listen.

Meanwhile, she'd keep her distance. She'd seen the bag he'd packed. When he'd gone to brush his teeth, she'd slipped a tracker inside.

It was almost too easy.

Now she just needed to bide her time until she went after him.

She hadn't been able to sleep anyway, so she went to the stables. She stopped by Winnie, her favorite horse.

Winnie had been a winning racehorse until an injury knocked her out of the running. Her owner lost interest and sold her. That's when Charlie bought Winnie and brought her here to nurse her back to health and wellness.

Winnie was probably Sienna's favorite because she could relate.

Sometimes Sienna also felt as if she'd been discarded—like everything she'd worked so hard to achieve had been meaningless.

That realization still hurt at times.

But she'd found a home here.

When Charlie had picked her for this assignment, Sienna knew she couldn't say no.

What they were doing here at Vanishing Ranch was important. Even though she'd never seen herself as a ranch hand, she'd found she enjoyed it.

Sienna brushed the mare a few minutes. But Winnie wasn't the horse she would take out.

Sienna would need her strongest, most reliable male for this trip. That would be Amigo, a chestnut Shire who was capable of carrying up to three hundred pounds, plus the weight of the saddle.

Thankfully, Sienna didn't weigh that much, and Jesse probably only weighed a hundred seventy pounds.

She glanced at the tracker again. Jesse had been walking almost an hour now, and he appeared to be about four miles away.

In another half hour, he'd reach the base of the mountains.

He probably had no clue what kind of creatures waited for him there.

Creatures like rattlesnakes, mountain lions, and bobcats.

Sienna had been on a trail ride once when she scanned the rocky terrain around her. When she examined the area a second time, she noticed one of the boulders was gone.

Because it hadn't been a boulder.

It had been a mountain lion waiting to pounce.

Thankfully, she'd been on her ATV, and she'd outrun it.

But she'd heard of others who hadn't been as lucky.

People who didn't know the dangers of this terrain shouldn't mess with it.

She'd tried to tell Jesse that, but he hadn't listened.

Sienna unlocked the nine-foot-tall iron gate and prodded Amigo with her heel, guiding him outside the fenced perimeter. The gate quietly closed behind her as she headed out to retrieve her missing hostage.

She wasn't in a hurry. As long as she caught up to Jesse before he reached the mountains, she'd be happy.

She checked her phone and noted Jesse's location.

She still had a little time to pace herself.

Her only worry was that she wouldn't be able to convince Jesse to come back with her. He was just stubborn enough to say no.

Then what would she do? Follow him until he changed his mind?

But she didn't have that kind of time—not when people were dying.

Sienna had to figure out a way to get through to Jesse—not just about coming back to the ranch but about helping her with this assignment.

CHAPTER
SEVEN

JESSE REACHED FOR HIS SIDE, for the stitches there—stitches that felt tight and reminded him of injuries he couldn't remember.

He knew this would be an arduous walk, but it was even harder than he'd anticipated.

His body was screaming with pain and clearly not ready for this kind of physical activity. His muscles were already sore. His bones ached. Despite the cooler nighttime temperatures, he was hot and thirsty. It didn't matter how much water he drank, he still felt parched.

It didn't matter. Jesse didn't have any other choice but to move forward.

He'd served for six years in the military, and some of those years had even been in the Middle East. The nighttime landscape surrounding him reminded

Jesse of being over there. At least, the moon was out right now, casting some soft light on his way.

Just keep putting one foot in front of the other.

Was the mountain getting farther away?

Jesse knew it couldn't be. But it seemed like it.

He felt himself getting weak. Despite that, he refused to stop. He couldn't give himself a break, even if that was what his body needed.

He had to see if he could cross this mountain range before the sun began to rise. He needed to remain concealed. It was his best chance of escaping.

Something moved in the distance, and he froze.

Someone—or something—was out there.

Could it be some type of critter on the prowl?

Whatever it was, it was in front of him, not behind.

Suddenly, Jesse realized what a bad idea this was. He didn't know what had happened in the past week. But he knew—even before recent events—that he had his fair share of enemies.

And what if there was a mole inside the FBI?

Another noise sounded.

Closer this time.

He slowly rounded a rocky outcropping and spotted a small fire blazing in the center of a ring of rocks. A man sat in front of it.

A man?

Could this be his chance to find help?

He quickly contemplated his options.

He could skirt around the guy and keep walking. But how long could he keep going?

This guy could be his only chance of getting away from this place.

"Excuse me," Jesse said as he stepped forward.

But as the man turned toward him, Jesse spotted a gun in the man's hands . . . a gun pointed directly at Jesse's chest.

"Don't move," the man ordered. "Put your hands up."

Sienna paused as she spotted Jesse in the distance. He stood still. Hands raised.

Something was wrong.

Then she saw a man standing with a gun glinting in the light of a small fire.

She frowned. She was going to need to handle things a little differently than she'd anticipated.

Vagrants sometimes liked to hang out in the desert—either looking for trouble or hiding from it.

Apparently, Jesse had just walked right into the path of one.

Sienna climbed from Amigo and tied the reins to

a nearby Joshua tree. Then she clutched her rifle, circled around, and approached the man from behind.

The man had long hair pulled back into a sloppy ponytail, as well as a scraggly beard. He wore cut-off jean shorts and a stained T-shirt, along with sandals. A ratty backpack—and that gun—appeared to be his only belongings.

"I'd stop what I was doing if I were you and lower that gun," she muttered.

The man stiffened. "I'm just having a conversation."

"If that's the case, put your gun down," Sienna ordered.

He glanced over his shoulder at her, eyeing her weapon. "Only if you do."

She fired into the air. "Don't test me."

"Okay, okay!" The man slowly placed the gun in his backpack and took a step back. "I'm just looking for a little cash. I ain't planning to hurt no one. Besides, he's the one who came up to me."

"This guy here doesn't have any cash. Besides, you have far bigger problems right now. You need to leave before things turn really ugly."

The man scowled before muttering something beneath his breath and scooping up his backpack.

"Shoulda known a handsome fella like that would have a woman chasing after him."

"Chasing him, my foot . . ." Sienna rolled her eyes. "Now leave. I'm not moving until I see you disappear, and this gun will be pointed at you until you do. Do you understand?"

"Yeah, yeah."

"Show a lady some respect," Sienna mumbled. "Because I'm an entirely better shot than you are. Believe me."

The man gave her one last withering look before continuing on his way.

As he disappeared behind a hill, Sienna moved toward Jesse, her gun still raised toward the vagrant.

"Going out wasn't such a great idea, now, was it?" She didn't bother to soften her tone. She'd tried to warn Jesse, and he'd put himself at risk anyway. "Good thing I found you in time."

He narrowed his eyes, looking more annoyed than grateful. "I thought no one was around for twenty miles."

"I'm pretty sure we mentioned the vagrants around here. We can't patrol all two hundred acres of our property."

"How does someone just wander into such a remote area?"

"Some of them are hiding out. Some live out this

way. There are some caves in these mountains. Some live off the land as best they can. But most don't survive long out here without the basics of water and food. Or the wildlife gets to them. Any number of things can happen."

Jesse narrowed his gaze as he studied her. "You look pretty comfortable out here with that rifle."

He had no idea. "I am."

Sienna retrieved her horse and slid her rifle into the scabbard on the horse's saddle. "We need to get you back."

Jesse stilled, seeming to dig his heels in. "What if I don't want to get back?"

"I could start telling you again about all the dangers out here, starting with mountain lions and steep drop-offs and the chance that it could rain tonight. Did you know flash floods have been known to kill multiple people here every year during monsoon season? Not to mention there are thirty-six types of venomous rattlesnakes slithering around in this state. Let's see . . . there's the Southwestern speckled rattlesnake, the Mojave rattlesnake, the—"

"Fine." Jesse's eyebrows drew together. "You made your point."

"Good. I was hoping you'd see things my way. Come on, and Amigo will give us a ride back."

She led the horse closer and climbed on first. Then she motioned for Jesse to sit behind her.

Jesse stared at them skeptically. "You sure the horse can handle our weight?"

"Believe me, I picked Amigo just for this reason. He's a strong guy with a strong back. I'd make you walk before I hurt this horse."

"Noted." Jesse climbed onto Amigo and flung his leg to the other side before sitting as far away from her as possible.

"You're going to have to scoot closer, cowboy."

Sienna figured that Jesse had a ready retort, but he held his tongue. It was too bad—she rather enjoyed ribbing him.

Instead, he sighed before scooting closer just as she'd told him.

"Put your arms around my waist," she said. "Don't be shy. We *are* married, after all."

Jesse paused before wrapping his hands around her. He squeezed tighter than she expected. Probably on purpose to try to throw her off her game.

But that task was nearly impossible. Jesse would learn that soon.

Maybe this would be the moment that clicked in place in his mind.

She could only hope at least.

CHAPTER
EIGHT

AS JESSE CAUGHT a sniff of Sienna's sunflower scent, something about the aroma made him want to lean closer.

But he didn't.

It wouldn't be appropriate.

Even if she was *technically* his wife.

He scowled at the thought of it.

How had his life gotten to this point?

And the even bigger question—what was he going to do about it?

Sienna led the horse back to the ranch, their bodies bouncing along with the animal's gait. The woman certainly knew how to handle herself atop this stallion and over this landscape.

"So, what happens if I do this?" he asked. "Once

this mission is over, you know I'm going to arrest you, right?"

"You can try. If that's what you want to do."

"And what about this so-called marriage that the two of us are bound to?"

She shrugged. "You *could* just stay here where it's safe when this is all done."

He heard something waver in her voice. He was sure of it.

The first crack in her pretense.

Was she at the ranch because it provided safety? Did Sienna have some kind of story she hid behind her sassy façade?

Jesse's curiosity about the woman only continued to grow.

"Or?" he clarified.

"Or . . . I can make sure all the paperwork concerning our marriage disappears, and it will be like it never happened."

Now *that* sounded like a plan. "Really? You can do that?"

"I have my connections." She shrugged as if it weren't a big deal.

"Just like that? You'd agree to dissolve our union so quickly? Ouch, that hurts." Jesse didn't know where the quip had come from. It almost sounded flirtatious. That was *not* what he'd intended.

"Believe it or not, I never wanted to get married in the normal sense. I don't want the drama that comes with it. So being married to you is perfect. Because we're married, but we're not. There are no joint checking accounts, no expectations, no pressure to make future decisions together. It's nothing but a contract."

"And you're really okay with that?" Jesse had never in his life met a woman who'd only wanted a marriage on paper.

A brief moment of silence passed, the only sound that of Amigo's hooves hitting the dry, dusty ground as they headed back toward the ranch.

"I'm more than okay with that," Sienna said. "It's ideal actually."

Jesse frowned. There was clearly more to her story.

And he wanted to know what.

Did it work? Sienna wondered as they bounced over the terrain heading back to the ranch. Had she convinced Jesse to go along with their scheme?

It almost sounded like he was considering her plan.

Either way, he needed to be grateful Sienna had gotten to him when she did tonight.

Otherwise, he could be hurt right now—even more than he already was—and left out here without anyone to help him.

She knew what that was like.

But she didn't dare tell him that. The more walls she kept up, the better.

At the gate, she punched in her code and then they trotted inside the compound.

Jesse had been surprisingly quiet the past several minutes, so she let him have his space.

No doubt, he had a lot to think about.

She nudged Amigo, and he stopped by the stable. Jesse hopped off first. Surprisingly, he offered her his hand and helped her down.

Probably just an automatic gentlemanly response.

Still, something about it caused a surge of warmth to flood her.

She quickly shoved the feeling down.

Instead, hanging onto the horse's reins, she turned toward Jesse. "Can I trust that you'll stay here?"

"Yes, ma'am."

She raised her eyebrows. "I like the sound of that."

"I bet you do," he said dryly.

Sienna leaned closer. "Even if you try to leave again, you know I have people watching you, right?"

"That's what I guessed." He rubbed his jaw, clearly annoyed.

"So, you might as well sleep on this. We can talk again in the morning." She started into the stable to put Amigo away.

"Sienna?"

She paused and glanced back at Jesse. "Yes?"

"What if I say no? If I refuse to go along with any of this?"

Her heart pounded in her ears.

What if he *did* say no? What would she do then?

No wasn't an option. Jesse was their best chance at getting the answers they needed.

She swallowed hard before saying, "Then we'll have to kill you."

She was only joking.

But Jesse didn't need to know that.

CHAPTER
NINE

THEN WE'LL HAVE *to kill you.*

The statement hadn't stopped echoing in Jesse's mind since Sienna had made the declaration last night.

He was *definitely* stuck in the middle of nowhere with a bunch of psychopaths.

Now he had to figure out what to do about it.

He'd awoken at the crack of dawn—not by choice. A rooster had been right outside his window.

All night, he'd had fuzzy dreams. Dreams that included beeping heart monitors, the smell of anti-septic cleaner, the sound of people murmuring around him.

Memories of his time in the hospital were probably trying to surface. Hopefully he'd remember something significant soon.

Hudson was already gone by the time Jesse's eyes had popped open. Jesse had prided himself in being more alert than that. But maybe everything that had happened was messing with his mind and well-being.

He quickly dressed in a clean set of cowboy clothes that had been left out for him.

How thoughtful.

If only these people didn't want to kill him.

He stepped outside and, against his better instincts, paused in awe.

Just beyond the mountains in the distance the sun rose, bigger and brighter than any sunrise he ever remembered seeing before. Pink rimmed the top of the mountains followed by a deep purple and then light blue filled the sky. There wasn't a cloud in sight.

This area . . . it was breathtaking. For a moment, Jesse felt grateful for this view.

Even if he was here against his will.

He strode across the dusty ground, ignoring a lizard scrabbling across the dirt toward a nearby plant. Even from a distance, he smelled the scent of sizzling bacon coming from the mess hall, and his stomach rumbled in response.

As he stepped onto the terra-cotta tile floor, cool air rushed around him. The dining hall, decorated in a Southwestern décor, greeted him along with eight heavy wooden tables and chairs.

A woman with a girl, probably eight years old, sat at another table eating and looking at what appeared to be a coloring book. They weren't dressed like everyone else here, but instead wore black pants and frilly shirts.

They weren't staying in the bunkhouse. Maybe one of the cabanas?

The woman glanced up at him, momentary fear flashing in her gaze.

Jesse's breath caught.

Were those two here against their will also?

His gaze shifted, and he spotted Sienna across the room looking over some papers at one of the tables.

She flashed him a deceitfully sweet smile before standing and striding his way.

He just couldn't figure this woman out.

Then again, maybe that's exactly what she wanted—to keep him on his toes and confused.

"How did you sleep?" She paused in front of him, her head tilting up toward him.

Jesse hadn't realized until this moment how much taller he was. He stood at six foot two, and he'd guess Sienna was at least a foot shorter. Yet she carried herself almost like a giant.

He ran a hand through his hair. "All things considered, I guess I'm doing fine."

She punched him on the side of the arm playfully. "That's what I like to hear, cowboy. Now, how about we get you something to eat? It's going to be a busy day."

"Busy day? What exactly did you have in mind for today?"

His foiled escape plan had proven that Jesse wasn't ready for too much physical activity. His injuries needed to heal more first.

At the thought, he reached for his rib cage again. He liked to think of himself as being tough. But falling from that roof had clearly taken a toll on him.

He didn't want any more drama. Not right now at least. All he wanted at the moment was to eat.

With that thought in mind, he joined Sienna at the table for breakfast.

At least, Jesse was in good spirits this morning, Sienna mused.

She hadn't been sure if he'd wake up with another chip on his shoulder and try to run again or not. But she was pleasantly surprised he hadn't.

She observed him another moment as he sat

across from her eating eggs, bacon, and a biscuit that Chef had served.

The man actually looked good as a cowboy, even though Jesse seemed to prefer the city slicker look, that tough and cool aura he gave off as an under-cover FBI agent.

But . . . he looked like a natural cowboy.

Not that he'd care.

Sienna had already eaten so she simply took a sip of her coffee and studied him.

After he took a few bites of his bacon, he paused and tilted his head. "Are you just going to watch me eat?"

She shrugged. "I'm just giving you space."

He quirked an eyebrow. "This is what you call space?"

Sienna wanted to laugh, but she didn't. "This is my version of space."

"Very well then." He took another bite of his bacon before washing it down with some coffee.

"I need to go over a few things with you this morning," she finally started.

"I have nowhere to go, and no choice but to listen, so go right ahead."

A small amount of guilt pricked her conscience at his words. She wanted to argue with him, but she couldn't.

Jesse would probably never believe this, but she liked a fair fight. That *probably* wasn't what this would be considered. But there was no other way to convince him to help with this assignment.

So, she'd been reduced to this.

"I need you to go with me to Phoenix tomorrow," she announced.

"And how far away is Phoenix?" He took another bite of bacon.

"It depends. If we take back roads, it's about two and a half hours. Or if you prefer the interstate and something a little less adventurous—for the sake of your ribs—then it'll be about three and a half hours."

"I think my ribs can handle the shorter trip."

"The road is pretty rocky. But it's also a lot of fun."

He narrowed his eyes. "What exactly are we going to do in Phoenix?"

"I want you to arrange a meeting for both of us with Blaine Benning."

His eyebrows shot up in surprise. "My sister's ex-boyfriend?"

"That's right. The two of you still stay in touch, right?"

His chewing slowed. "Yes, we do. But I don't understand where you're going with this."

This was where it got complicated. Sienna

couldn't say too much. Not until she knew if she could trust Jesse or not. Right now, that was still uncertain.

"I need to talk to Blaine and figure out if he has some intel that we need," she shared.

"Some intel? What are you? CIA or something?"

She let out a short laugh.

If he only knew.

"That's not important," Sienna said instead. "I just need an in with him, and you're the perfect guy."

"So, that's the entire reason that you grabbed me? Because of Blaine?"

"It's complicated," she said.

"You keep saying that."

"Only because it's true."

Jesse narrowed his eyes. "And this has something to do with the botched army operation you mentioned earlier? As well as the three dead people?"

"That's correct. That army operation . . . it actually involved Blaine's uncle . . . Major Roger Benning."

"Major Benning? He's a good man. I won't let you rake his name through the mud."

"I didn't say that's what we were going to do. We're still trying to find the information we need."

Jesse stared at her, not saying anything. But she saw the wheels turning in his mind.

She wasn't going to give him the chance to say no.

"There are a few things we need to go over before we leave—including a cover story," she told him.

"This ought to be good." His familiar scowl returned.

"Oh, it will be." Sienna nodded. "But you'll want to finish eating first because you'll need your energy today."

CHAPTER
TEN

JESSE DIDN'T LIKE the sound of any of this, but he had no choice other than to act like he was okay with the way things were playing out right now.

Maybe in Phoenix he'd find the opportunity to run. He *was* an FBI agent. He was fully capable of getting out of situations like this.

At least, that's what he'd thought until he'd come here. After last night's escapade, maybe that wasn't completely true.

"The horses need tending to," Sienna said after breakfast. "Let's talk more as we work."

He followed her out to the stables.

"So, this is simply a working ranch where you rescue horses?" He needed some clarification, trying to put together the pieces.

She shrugged. "Something like that. These horses

. . . some of them had to disappear. Their owners aren't exactly taking care of them very well, so we see to it that they're taken care of in the way that they should be."

"So, you steal them?"

"That sounds so illegal when you say it that way."

"That's because it *is* illegal."

"Potato, *potato*." She flashed a grin. "Anyway, Charlie has a real heart for these horses. We're only trying to look out for their best interest."

Jesse wasn't sure if it was admirable or not, but he kept his mouth shut.

"Some are injured. Others are neglected. A few have been abandoned. Each of them has a story." Sienna handed him a brush and nodded toward one of the stalls. "That's Tucker over there. He needs to be brushed, so make yourself useful while I brush Winnie." She gestured toward the mare.

"Yes, ma'am." He took the brush and began stroking it across Tucker's back.

"Wait one second." Sienna stepped closer, her hand covering his as she stroked the brush away from the horse's face, guiding his hand. "You don't want to rub Tucker the wrong way—literally or figuratively."

"This way?" He followed the hair in the direction

it grew, trying to ignore the burst of pleasure that rushed through him at Sienna's touch, at her closeness.

This woman was such a mystery, and he wanted to know more about her.

And another part of him wanted to relish her sweet scent. Her silky hair as it skimmed his jaw. The soft skin of her hand against his.

"Perfect." Sienna stepped back and supervised him a minute.

As quickly as it had started, the moment ended, and Jesse instantly missed her nearness—something he had no business enjoying.

Wife or not.

The horse neighed in pleasure, and Jesse had to suppress a smile to hide his delight. Who knew such a simple act could bring an animal so much happiness?

"How long have you been here?" Jesse asked as he continued brushing. Maybe this was his opportunity to get some information.

"A year."

"What did you do before you were a ranch hand and professional kidnapper?"

She flinched as if his words had hit a soft spot. "I worked for the government."

"That's pretty broad."

She nodded. "I know."

Jesse got the message. Sienna didn't want to share any more details with him. It wasn't surprising.

"But I know quite a bit about you," she continued, clearly deflecting the subject back to something she was more comfortable with—him. "You joined the military right out of high school. You stayed in for six years. Then the FBI recruited you."

"You've done your research." It wasn't an accusation. He could admire a woman that took charge.

"The FBI probably recruited you because you were exemplary in your service as well as selfless." Sienna started brushing Winnie as she spoke. "In fact, you were willing to sacrifice yourself for your colleagues on more than one occasion. Very admirable. You joined the FBI and have been a part of them for the past ten years. But most of your time has been undercover. It's easy to lose yourself in those kinds of situations."

Jesse cast a glance at her when he heard her serious tone. "You sound like you know from experience."

She shrugged and continued to brush Winnie.

When she didn't offer any more information, he said, "Well, you have my dossier down pat."

"That's part of what I do."

"This is all very interesting, but I thought we were going to talk about Phoenix."

She paused and lowered her brush as she turned toward him. "Yes, Phoenix. We're going to need to make sure we have our cover story correct. Otherwise, Blaine will never trust me, and our time will be wasted."

Sienna had known Jesse Marx would be sharp. But he was picking up on entirely more than she was comfortable with.

That's why she needed to keep the focus on him instead of her.

She didn't want him to know about her past with the CIA. About how she understood perfectly what it was like to be undercover. To feel as if she'd disappeared and was just a shell of the person she'd once been.

None of those things were important right now.

All that was important was finding the answers they needed.

And speaking with Blaine Benning was their next step.

She and Monroe could have cornered Blaine on

their own, without Jesse. They could have forced Blaine to talk under duress.

But that wasn't what Charlie wanted.

They needed a better approach. They needed to find someone Blaine would trust and see if they could get information that way.

So that's exactly what they were going to do.

"Tell me a little about Blaine." Sienna leaned against the rough wooden door of the stall.

Jesse shrugged and stepped back, rolling the sleeves of his plaid shirt up higher and revealing muscular forearms.

Very nice forearms.

Since when did she notice someone's forearms?

Since now, apparently.

She forced herself to look away. Forced herself not to think about the spark of electricity she'd felt as she'd helped Jesse brush the horse. As their hands had touched. As they'd leaned into each other.

"I don't know what kind of information you're looking for," Jesse told her. "Blaine is a nice guy, and so is his uncle."

"Why did he and your sister break up?"

"Blaine was in the army, and I don't think my sister liked that kind of life. She wanted someone who was there for her more. The breakup was amicable. It's the only reason I was able to remain friends with Blaine."

"When's the last time you talked to him?"

Jesse let out a sigh and paused with the brush in hand. "Oh, I don't know. It's probably been three years, at least. It's hard to talk to friends and family and keep up with them when you're undercover most of the time."

A frown flickered at the corner of her lips. "I'm sure that's hard. Has it been hard on your family?"

He nodded as his gaze clouded. "It has been. The undercover assignment with the cartel was my last one. I want out. I'm ready for something new."

Sienna studied him a moment, wondering what exactly had happened.

When he didn't say anything or offer any more information, she said, "Well, you almost died before that wish came true."

"But you showed up right in time like my knight in shining armor." A hint of humor edged his voice.

"More like your knight in a shiny dump truck."

His lips twitched, almost as if he wanted to smile. But he didn't. "So, it was you driving the truck? I guess I should thank you . . ."

Before she could respond, her phone buzzed. As she glanced at it, her breath caught.

A friend with the FBI had texted her.

The feds had circulated an internal memo marking Jesse as a person of interest.

Whoever had stabbed Jesse in the back was now making sure people thought he was a traitor.

That was going to make all this even more complicated.

"Everything okay?" Jesse asked.

She quickly put her phone away and nodded. "Of course. Let's get finished up in here. But we still have a lot more to talk about."

CHAPTER
ELEVEN

JESSE AND SIENNA had discussed things ad nauseam for the past three hours. They'd gotten their cover story down. Sienna had helped him pick out his clothing for the trip. He'd made a call to make sure he could meet with Blaine.

Jesse was just going along with everything like a good, obedient soldier.

Except he wasn't.

He'd never liked playing exactly by the rules, which was why working undercover had been his chosen assignment for so long.

He couldn't stop thinking about the look he'd seen on Sienna's face when she checked her phone. She knew more than she was letting on, didn't she?

Somehow, he needed to figure out what that information was.

For the last hour, they'd reviewed everything Sienna knew about the three dead men.

Nathan Rosson, thirty-eight, worked as a delivery driver in Idaho Falls. He was killed in a car accident a month ago.

Steve McIntosh, forty, owned a vending machine company in Pennsylvania. He'd died when a home invasion turned deadly three weeks ago.

Isaac Wells, thirty-five, worked for a military contractor in Norfolk, Virginia. He succumbed to a mysterious illness last week.

The only thing that connected them all was the squadron they'd served on together fifteen years prior. Local law enforcement hadn't made the connection between the deaths. Sienna didn't sound hopeful that their theory would be taken seriously, even if they did come forward with that link.

Jesse had to admit that her case was compelling.

Afterward, he and Sienna had lunch, which was also hearty—chili, baked potatoes, and cornbread. Entirely heartier than what he was used to. If he wasn't careful, he would walk away from this place ten pounds heavier than when he'd come.

That was *if* Jesse did indeed walk away from this.

He still had his doubts.

Which was why he was keeping his eyes open for an escape plan.

As Sienna printed something in an office to the side of the mess hall, he saw his opportunity.

Her cell phone rested on the edge of the desk.

If Jesse could grab it, he could call for help. Call one of his colleagues or a friend or his sister even. Anyone.

But he had to wait for the right moment.

He lingered in the doorway, his arms crossed as he watched Sienna work.

The woman was a sight to see. Even though she'd abducted him, she was still strangely fascinating.

Which wasn't something he thought he would ever say.

But she was pretty and as smart as a whip with an accent that would make anyone think she was the sweetest gal this side of the Rio Grande.

But he saw something in her eyes. A certain cunningness.

What exactly did Sienna and Monroe want Jesse to find out from Blaine?

There was clearly more to the story than they let on.

As Sienna turned to grab something from the printer, Jesse quietly stepped forward.

He snatched the phone from the desk and slid it into his back pocket before she could see him.

His heart beat harder and sweat threatened to break out across his forehead.

Play it cool, he told himself. *That's what you do best.*

It was the only way he hadn't been caught in any of his undercover assignments all these years—until that last one, at least.

In fact, some of his colleagues had started to call him Slick. He never liked that nickname.

However, it was better than cowboy and hubby, which was what Sienna had taken to calling him.

He was hyper aware of the cell phone in his pocket. Anyone looking at him from behind would see the imprint of it. But there was nowhere else he could put the device where it wouldn't be seen.

He'd need to be careful. At his first opportunity, he'd make that call for help.

Maybe he'd actually get out of this place and away from this loony woman.

Sienna turned toward him, her eyes sparkling.

"Okay, now that we have this worked out, I want to rehearse our story together one more time today. We'll also have plenty of time to rehearse it on the drive to Phoenix tomorrow."

"Sounds good." Maybe Jesse shouldn't sound so compliant. But he just needed a moment by himself.

Then maybe he'd be free from this desert prison.

Sienna watched as Jesse lowered himself into the seat across from her desk. He was being surprisingly easy to get along with right now.

Which made her suspicious.

They spent the next several minutes going over their cover story again to make sure it sounded believable. They couldn't risk anyone picking up on the fact they were lying.

As a part of the cover story, Sienna would pose as Jesse's wife.

That meant he'd need to look a little more comfortable around her.

However, she wasn't exactly sure that was even possible. The man acted as if he hated her right now.

Not that she could blame him. Still, something about that realization caused a surprising surge of disappointment to rise in her.

Regardless . . . the best thing they could do was to spend more time together.

Halfway through the conversation, he rose. "If it's okay, I'm going to use your restroom before we keep going."

Sienna stared at him before nodding. "Of course."

He rose from his seat and stepped toward the door.

There was one more thing she needed to tell him. "Jesse?"

He paused as he faced her. "Yes?"

She held out her hand. "I'm going to need my cell phone back before you go to the bathroom."

She grinned.

Jesse had thought she hadn't noticed, hadn't he?

If that was the case, then Jesse was entirely under-estimating her.

If there was one thing Sienna hated it was being underestimated.

CHAPTER
TWELVE

AS JESSE HANDED the phone back to Sienna, he tried to control his frustration.

But he was failing.

How had Sienna seen him take that phone? He hadn't made a sound, and he'd kept his back away from her so she wouldn't see the imprint in his jeans.

She'd known anyway.

The last thing he wanted was to set up Blaine or Blaine's uncle. They were good guys. Whatever Sienna thought she knew about them, she was wrong.

No way would Jesse backstab a friend like that.

He was trying to play nice but losing his patience.

Soon, he'd have to take drastic measures.

As the two of them left the office, he glanced around in the empty mess hall.

He didn't even hear Chef clanking around in the kitchen.

He slowed his steps as a mix of curiosity and suspicion filled him. "Where is everyone?"

"They had to go into town to pick up some supplies. Why?" She headed toward the outside door.

Jesse's thoughts began to race. "I was just wondering."

Sienna grunted softly as if she didn't believe him.

But he knew this could be his window of opportunity.

His mom had taught him to never lay a finger on a woman.

And, normally, Jesse abided by that.

But Sienna was *not* a normal woman. She was clearly trained and dangerous. Had she been sent by one of his enemies? Was this whole situation just some kind of test?

Maybe.

Maybe not.

If Jesse didn't act soon, he could very well end up dead.

"I know you're probably getting tired," Sienna said as she detoured from the exit toward another door tucked away in the corner. "But I wanted to show you our workout room just in case you ever need to blow off steam. Although, the term *workout room* is probably an exaggeration. Charlie loves kickboxing, so there are several punching bags and a workout mat in there."

"Good to know." But Jesse wasn't paying attention to those details.

If he was going to act, he needed to act now before everybody else came back. His muscles bristled with anticipation.

"It's right in here." She pushed the door open.

But as soon as Sienna stepped inside, Jesse needed to make his move. It was now or never.

Acting quickly, Jesse stepped in behind her. Before she could turn toward him, he grabbed her arms with one hand, pinning them behind her. He put her into a headlock with his other hand.

"Look at you, being all quick on the draw like that," Sienna muttered. "Impressive."

"I'm not playing games with you," Jesse growled. "You're going to give me your car keys, and I'm going to drive away from this place. Do I make myself clear?"

"Yes, whatever you want. Just don't hurt me."

The words didn't even sound right coming from Sienna's lips.

He should have known.

The next instant, she pivoted.

Jesse flew over her shoulder and landed on the floor.

More pain ripped through his ribs, but at least he'd landed on the mat.

"I wish you hadn't made me do that." Sienna crouched in fighting position in front of him.

Who *was* this woman?

He pushed aside his pain and popped to his feet, fisting his hands in front of him, ready for a fight. "You can't keep me here."

"I don't want to keep you here against your wishes. I just want to change your mind and have you work with me—*willingly*. But you're being very difficult."

They began circling each other. "I wonder why."

"We need your help. That's all we're asking."

"What you're asking is for me to sell out one of my friends. To stay here against my will. To forsake my freedom in favor of marrying you—something I apparently had no choice in."

She shrugged stiffly and shook her head. "That was the only way to save you. You need to understand that."

"I don't understand anything." Before they could talk any longer, Jesse charged toward her.

But Sienna was quick on her feet. She somehow ducked and flipped him over again onto his back.

More pain ripped through his abdomen.

How had she known to do that?

One thing was for sure.

Escaping was going to be a lot harder than he ever anticipated.

———

Sienna should have known this was coming. If she was in Jesse's shoes, she'd do the same thing right now.

She turned back to face him, still poised to fight. She almost felt bad for the guy as he lay on the floor, his agony obvious. Fighting like this wasn't a good idea with his injuries. She hoped he hadn't pulled any stitches.

"I didn't want to do that," she told him. "But you didn't leave me any choice."

He dragged himself back to his feet. Instead of responding, he just let out a grunt. His gaze made it clear he wasn't giving up yet.

Jesse sure was a stubborn one.

Sienna fought a sigh. "We don't have to do this."

"If you think that I'm just going to do whatever you say without a fight, then you're wrong."

"I'd hoped you wouldn't say that." She braced herself, anticipating his next move.

What he didn't know was that Sienna had been trained with the best of the best. She was no amateur and had depended on her skills to stay alive on more than one occasion.

Jesse lunged for her again.

But this time he surprised her and grabbed her arm.

Before she could swipe her leg behind her and knock Jesse off his feet, he twisted her arm until it felt like it might break. Then he pushed her against the wall.

Sienna knew how to get out of this situation.

But she didn't need to let him know that—not yet at least.

As he held her in place, she was all too aware of his muscular frame behind her. Not that she was surprised. When she'd rescued him, she'd noticed his well-defined muscles. She'd known the man was strong.

Feeling his body heat did something funny to her pulse. It wasn't just the situation that had her blood racing.

It was Jesse Marx.

She had no business feeling anything for this

man. But maybe, just for a moment, she could enjoy this predicament.

He leaned close enough that she could feel his breath in her ear. "Now, wifey . . . I need you to tell me what's really going on here."

Sienna cringed as he put more pressure on her arm. "There are easier ways to do things, you know."

"I'm not stupid. I saw the way you handled that gun yesterday. I noticed the way you're fighting today. Are you FBI too?"

She narrowed her eyes, fighting the pain. But Jesse had her trapped a little too well right now. "I'm not FBI."

"Military intelligence?"

"I was CIA, okay?" It pained Sienna to say the words. She didn't like to talk about her former career. And she definitely didn't like to tell strangers.

"You're a spook?"

"I prefer the term 'operative.'"

"Are you guys trying to trick me by bringing me here? Is this a test?"

She clenched her teeth. "No, I'm not CIA anymore. I work for a private agency now."

"This ranch is a cover for something, isn't it?"

Sienna hesitated, not wanting to tell Jesse the truth.

But she knew that Jesse wasn't going to let her go without some answers, and she didn't want to give away all her secrets just yet. She'd allow him to think he'd bested her.

For now.

CHAPTER
THIRTEEN

JESSE FINALLY FELT as if he was onto something.

He didn't want to hurt Sienna.

Not at all.

But she wouldn't give him any answers unless he fought back like this.

So, he continued to hold her in place against the wall. He ignored the aching in his own rib cage. He'd deal with that later.

This situation . . . it was a matter of life or death. *His* life or death.

He leaned closer to Sienna, ready to drive home his questions—and let her know he was in control now. "I asked if this ranch was a cover for something else."

"Kind of." Her voice sounded strained through her clenched teeth.

But Jesse didn't dare let her off the hook. "Keep going."

"We really do take care of horses that need our help. But we take on other assignments also."

"Like what?"

She let out a small sigh. "We help people disappear."

"What?" Jesse's mind raced through what she was telling him.

He remembered the woman and child sitting at that table at breakfast. He recalled the fear in the woman's gaze.

Suddenly, the name Vanishing Ranch took on an entirely different meaning.

Were these people really trying to help women and children? Or was this all some kind of human trafficking organization? If that was the case, he needed to figure out a way to do something.

"Sometimes people need to get away for some reason or another," Sienna continued. "Mostly, we take in women in abusive relationships. We bring them here to help them disappear and to give them a new identity as well as the skills they need to move forward."

He soaked in those new details. "How do you even find these women?"

"We have a network, mostly with various women's shelters and former law enforcement. They let us know when someone is desperate and has exhausted all other means possible. As you know, women like that can't go into witness protection. Often, they're left without any means or possibilities. They feel trapped. No woman should feel that way."

"You let them stay here? Or is this just a place where they pass through?" Questions continued to pummel him.

"We give them a new life. New IDs, new skills, new backgrounds. We train them for various situations they may encounter. We counsel them. We let them help with the horses—and sometimes in helping other abused creatures, that helps them find healing in themselves also. There's no timeline for their stay. We make sure they're well equipped before they start their new lives."

Jesse didn't want to admire this place, but if what Sienna said was true then it sounded like the people who worked here were doing a good thing.

But it still didn't make sense why they'd grabbed him.

He pressed in closer, trying to ignore the alluring scent of her sunflower perfume.

He could not let himself get distracted right now —even if her hair did feel silky against his cheek.

"So, are you trying to make me disappear?" he growled.

"No. We never intended for things to turn out this way, but we had to make some quick decisions. That's how you and I ended up married, and you eventually woke up here. We didn't mean any harm by it. That's the truth."

She sounded sincere. But she could be a great actress, an expert at manipulation.

"What other reasons did you have for grabbing me?" he asked.

"Aside from your excellent undercover skills, your ability to craft a new persona and infiltrate organizations, and your years of tactical training?" She shrugged. "We *did* hear from one of our contacts that you're the *crème de la crème* when it comes to making fake IDs. That's what you did for the cartel, right?"

"Yes," he answered slowly, cautiously. "But I did it only because I was also able to give those fake IDs to the authorities to track. It was part of my under-cover assignment."

"The women who come here . . . they need to start new lives. You have the skills to help them do that."

He let that settle in his mind. It was going to take some time.

And Jesse couldn't hold Sienna like this all day.

Jesse leaned closer. "If I let you go, do you promise to be good?"

"I'll think about it."

His grip tightened.

"Okay, okay!" Her voice rose. "I'll be good."

After another moment of hesitation, he released Sienna. She turned and scowled at him as she shook out her muscles and rubbed her neck—clearly not appreciating what had just happened.

Jesse remained on guard as more questions pressed on him.

This whole situation was suddenly seeming far more interesting than it once had.

Sienna had known there would come a moment when she needed to tell Jesse everything. First, she wanted to know she could trust him.

But given the way the situation had played out, she hadn't had much choice. Besides . . . she hadn't told him *everything*—just enough to let him think he had the upper hand and to give him the illusion of control.

Now Sienna hoped she could trust the man with what she'd said.

He still stared at her, that brooding, street-wary look in his gaze. "Are you in any way working with the Campeche Cartel?"

She scoffed. "The cartel? Please. Why would I ever want to work with those dirtbags?"

"You're really not that much different than they are. You kidnapped me. You're keeping me here against my will. Forcing me to do things that I don't want to do."

"We're simply trying to persuade you." She raised her chin.

"But it's like you said last night, if I say no, you'll kill me."

Amusement fluttered through her gaze. "I was only joking."

He scowled. "That's not funny."

She shrugged. "I can see that now. Sorry."

Jesse ran his hand through his hair. "There are better ways to do things. You do realize that, don't you? I need to talk to your boss. Charlie."

"You can't right now."

"Why not?"

"Charlie's out on an assignment for another two days. But when that's over, the two of you can chat."

He let out an exasperated sigh. "At that point, we'll have already gone to Phoenix."

"I know this doesn't seem ideal. I really do. But we wouldn't have gone through all this trouble to bring you here unless it was important. Can we at least just make a truce until after our meeting with Blaine tomorrow? Then we can talk and maybe reevaluate. What do you say?" Sienna extended her hand.

Jesse stared at it a moment, appearing to contemplate his actions.

Then finally, he took her hand in his. "Deal. But at that point, if I want out, then I'm getting out. Am I clear?"

"As clear as a window after a washing."

He cast her a wry look.

Now Sienna just needed to convince Jesse to stay even when this was all over. They needed more help here, and Jesse would be perfect.

But what would it take for him to see that also?

———

A few hours later, Jesse stood near the fence, watching as Sienna rode Winnie, weaving in and out of some barrels in the center of a small arena-like area.

The woman was skilled . . . he'd give her that.

Monroe stood beside him, watching her work the horse. The sun was setting, easing up from spreading its brutal heat all over the ranch. Flies buzzed around them, and some birds were diving into the swimming pool in the distance.

The whole scene looked like something out of a movie.

"I know she may seem like a firecracker—not necessarily in a good way—but there's a lot more to Sienna than meets the eye," Monroe offered.

Jesse tried not to show his skepticism—but he was curious. "Is that right?"

"She's loyal to a fault. She and Charlie go way back."

The elusive Charlie again . . . Jesse was anxious to talk to the man when he returned.

Better yet, maybe Jesse would be long gone by then.

"Loyalty can be misplaced," Jesse finally said.

"Sienna would give her life to save a friend," Monroe said. "She's smart, she's quirky, and she's capable. She's someone you want on your side."

Jesse wasn't sure about that, but he kept the thought silent. He had other more pressing questions at the moment.

"Were you with Sienna when I fell from that

roof?" Jesse stepped back as Winnie kicked up some dust in front of them and the cloud floated their way. He was going to have to take another shower when all this was through.

"I was." Monroe's jaw jumped. "We had a source tell us what was about to go down. We followed you to that building, saw those men tail you inside, and we figured you might need some backup."

"But how did you know I'd end up on the roof?"

Monroe shrugged, his gaze still on Sienna. "We were following you, hoping to catch you alone. The cartel caught you alone first."

Jesse fought a frown. "So, who's idea was it to grab a dump truck?"

"It was just sitting there in the alley. So, we improvised. I'd say the big guy upstairs wants to keep you around for a while longer."

Jesse's eyebrows flickered up. "I guess He does."

"I know this is unconventional."

"To say the least." Jesse's eyebrows flickered toward the peach-colored sky, and he didn't bother to hold back his sarcasm.

"But there's a lot on the line. We did what we had to do to save you initially. That was our first priority. Then we brought you here to heal in hopes of convincing you to help us."

Jesse had opinions about all that, but he'd learned

there were times to be mouthy and times to stay quiet.

This was one of those quiet times.

"Jesse, this is bigger than you and me." Monroe finally looked away from Sienna and turned toward him. "We believe there's a high-level conspiracy going on and that multiple people have died as a direct result of it."

Monroe's words rang in Jesse's ears.

Was this real? He certainly sounded sincere.

But Jesse still needed to proceed with caution.

He glanced at Sienna again as she pulled on the reins and Winnie paced to a stop near them. Her face glowed with accomplishment as she glanced down at them, her cheeks flushed with exertion—and happiness.

"I think I'm making progress," she announced. "This has been good."

But Jesse wondered if she was talking about the horse or about him.

CHAPTER
FOURTEEN

THOUGH JESSE WAS STILL CAUTIOUS, he felt better hearing that Sienna was aboveboard.

Unless Monroe had been lying.

People who worked deep undercover became good liars. Jesse should know. And it sounded like Sienna had done just as much undercover work as Jesse had.

But his gut indicated Monroe's statement concerning Sienna's character was true.

Jesse only hoped his gut wasn't wrong.

After dinner, Jesse, Sienna, Hudson, and two other guys sat near a bonfire. Monroe strummed a guitar as they all gathered around.

Despite himself, Jesse almost found himself enjoying this moment.

He could get used to hanging out around a fire sharing memories and making s'mores.

It felt so normal. Normal was what he needed after spending so much time undercover and on guard. For so long, his entire life had revolved around being someone he wasn't. He'd nearly lost himself in the process. He'd forgotten what he really liked, the foods that were his favorites, what it was like to have true friendships. What he really wanted in life.

"Something about the nothingness of the desert helps me clear my head," Sienna leaned over and told him. "Somehow, it helps me feel like my life is more in focus."

She sounded so sincere that Jesse had to wonder if she was trying to pull one over on him again.

If this was all an act, then Sienna was good. Really good.

These people aren't your friends. Nothing about this situation is normal.

Jesse kept that reminder in the back of his mind.

Still, it was nice to let down his guard and pretend for a moment like his problems didn't exist.

Monroe started singing "Friends in Low Places," and Jesse leaned back, almost feeling relaxed.

"See? It's not that bad here." Sienna stared over at Jesse.

He only stared back, not inclined to give her any satisfaction—even if her words were true.

She had that same impish look in her gaze. Jesse had even grown to look forward to seeing it there.

Which made no sense.

The last thing he needed right now was to be attracted to this woman.

Then again, she *was* his wife.

Jesse let out a silent groan.

How would he navigate his way out of this one?

Certainly, the law had special clauses when it came to divorce, especially when you were married against your will. Even God had to give some allowances for that, right?

He sighed, unsure of the answers.

It didn't matter. He was running out of time.

When he woke up in the morning, he'd head to Phoenix to possibly betray someone he considered a friend.

Just how would he live with himself afterward?

After Jesse disappeared into the bunkhouse, Sienna waited around to talk to Monroe. They hadn't had a chance to catch up one-on-one, and she hadn't given him the latest updates yet.

He set his guitar back into its case then stood and turned to her. "How did today go?"

"Not great, but I think we made progress."

She told him about the day's events.

His jaw tightened. "I figured it was only a matter of time before he pulled another stunt. Do you think he'll honor your temporary truce?"

Sienna pressed her lips together before shaking her head. "I can't be sure, to be honest."

"Are you going to be okay being alone with him tomorrow?"

She waved her hand in the air. "I'll be fine. I can take care of myself."

"I know we all like to think that. But none of us are infallible."

His words caused her throat to tighten. He knew her story. Knew what she'd been through.

Even though there was wisdom in Monroe's statement, his words weren't what Sienna wanted to hear. She worked best when she compartmentalized. When she set aside her emotions and memories and focused on the task at hand.

But she also realized that wasn't the healthiest coping mechanism.

Sienna swallowed hard before saying, "If I need help, I'll let you know. I know you'll send someone."

"I will."

She shifted as she glanced at the fading embers of the bonfire. "How is Charlie?"

"Should be back tomorrow. The rescue seems to have been successful."

"That's good." The only reason Charlie wasn't here was because of that rescue.

Sienna glanced at the door leading to the bunkroom. Tomorrow was the big day, and she didn't want to blow it. So much was riding on this operation—so much more than even Jesse understood.

Yes, they needed to figure out why those three men had died. They needed to stop whoever was behind it before more people were killed.

But some people at this ranch had even more personal reasons to get involved—reasons Jesse didn't need to know about.

"I guess I should get to bed," she finally said.

"I'll have one of the guys stay out here tonight just in case Jesse tries anything. You need to get your sleep for your assignment tomorrow."

"Sounds good." But Sienna knew she wouldn't be getting much sleep either way. "I'll see you in the morning."

With that, Sienna slipped inside the bunkhouse

and prayed that tomorrow would be successful. They needed to talk to the rest of the men who'd been in this squadron in order to figure out why they might be getting killed off.

If they were too late, all those men might end up dead . . . along with their chances of finding answers.

CHAPTER
FIFTEEN

AS JESSE GOT ready the next morning, he still had reservations.

The good news was that he had his normal clothes back. It wouldn't bode well if he showed up to meet Blaine wearing cowboy boots and a chambray shirt. No, he needed to look like himself.

More dreams had haunted him last night. Blurry dreams of waking up to see an angel leaning over him smiling. The most gorgeous angel he'd ever seen telling him she would take care of him, that he would be okay.

He'd remembered muttering "I do" and feeling like the luckiest guy in the world.

Then he'd realized that angel was Sienna. In his hospital room. Persuading him to marry her.

More memories were resurfacing, he realized, biting back a frown.

He must have been on morphine.

Jesse stepped from the bunkhouse, backpack slung over his shoulder, and spotted Sienna waiting for him. She leaned against the side of the stable almost as if she'd known he would appear at any moment.

She straightened when she saw him, revealing form-fitting jeans, black boots, and a snug black T-shirt. She'd added a silver necklace, hoop earrings, and a touch of makeup.

The look . . . it was nice.

A little too nice.

Then again, Sienna had also looked nice in her dusty jeans, plaid shirt, and a cowboy hat.

He swallowed the lump in his throat before calling, "Morning."

"Morning, cowboy." She raised her eyebrows. "Although you don't look like much of a cowboy right now."

He straightened his leather jacket. "This is how I prefer to look."

"I kind of like both."

Her approval brought him a burst of unwanted pleasure. Why did he care what she thought? He didn't.

But his reaction said otherwise.

He'd have to figure that out later.

They fell into step beside each other as they headed toward the mess hall.

"Are you ready for today?" Sienna asked. "No cold feet?"

"No, I just want to get this over with. To be done and on my way."

"Are you trying to break a girl's heart?" Sienna placed a hand over her chest as if in emotional pain. "I thought we had a special connection."

Jesse rolled his eyes.

Was everything just an act for Sienna? Were any parts of her real?

He wasn't sure.

But he wanted to know who she was—who she *really* was. He wanted to know what had made her this way. What she was like when she let down her guard. What it would take to bring a genuine smile to her face.

He glanced at his watch. "It doesn't look like we have much time."

"I was thinking the same thing. Let's grab breakfast to go and then hit the road. I see you brought an overnight bag, just in case."

"I did."

"Perfect. Always be prepared. That's what I always say."

"You and every Boy Scout in America."

"I take that as a compliment." She flashed a grin.

Jesse resisted rolling his eyes again.

Here went nothing.

He had no idea how today would turn out . . . or how exactly he'd play his cards.

Sienna always enjoyed the ride from the ranch to Phoenix, especially when she took the shortcut.

Bouncing over the rocky road in her dust-coated white Jeep gave her a thrill.

Maybe that was why she'd gone to work for the CIA. She loved excitement.

At least, at one time in her life she had.

But after that last assignment . . . she wondered if it was time to move on and settle down. Then her old friend Charlie had offered her the job at the ranch.

Now here she was.

She prayed that today went well. She'd heard from one of her sources that the FBI had launched an internal investigation into Jesse. But since it was only internal, she didn't think the feds would track him down on the streets. Besides, he'd been stationed out of Las Vegas for his last assignment.

She hadn't told him that update on the internal investigation—she didn't want to give him the chance to get spooked. But that fact remained in the back of her mind, tucked away just in case something popped up.

"Tell me about this place in the middle of nowhere," Jesse said. "It's so entirely isolated. We haven't passed another house for miles."

"Isn't it great?"

"Depends on who you ask."

"This area . . . it's really no man's land. I mean, you can call 911, but it will probably take responders thirty minutes to get here. If you call the police directly? It could take even longer. So, people out here learn to do things their own way."

"You mean, take the law into their own hands?"

She shrugged as she gripped the steering wheel. "Maybe. But they have no other choice. There's no one to depend on but yourself and the people you surround yourself with. It's like the real Wild West, I suppose. I find it refreshing."

Jesse shifted. "One more question . . . the other guys on this squadron you mentioned . . . shouldn't you warn them?"

"There are four other men left. Stephen Gaston,

who lives near Phoenix. Carson Philips in Wyoming. Lee Blanco in Indiana. And the major. We have people stationed outside the homes of two of them."

"Why not the other two?"

"We're going to talk to the major personally. I'm also hoping to pay Stephen a visit while we're in town. We had someone sitting outside his place, but Stephen confronted him and asked him to leave."

"I see."

Sienna glanced out over the landscape as they cleared the mountain range and entered more of the Sonoran Desert. As soon as they crossed the range, the land flattened, and saguaro cactus appeared. The changes in scenery in this area seemed frequent and made it so there was always something new to see.

"I have to say, I didn't think places like this were left in America."

"It's pretty amazing, right?"

He didn't know how to answer that. "Sure, I guess."

An hour later, Sienna found a space in a parking garage in downtown Phoenix. But before they climbed from the Jeep, she turned to Jesse.

She could see the hesitation on his features, the reluctance to deceive someone he considered a friend. Compassion pounded inside her.

If there was another way . . . she wouldn't ask him to do this.

But there wasn't.

She cleared her throat, trying to push down her guilt. "Are you ready for this?"

Jesse shrugged. "Ready as I'll ever be."

"You're going to do great," Sienna told him—as if Jesse Marx needed encouragement. The man was undeterrable and acted as if he could conquer the world.

Maybe he could.

Sienna reached into her pocket and handed him something.

His eyebrows shot up when he saw his phone in her hand. "You trust me enough to give me this?"

"Not really. But you might need it. I just put the battery back in, but it should work."

He slipped the phone into his pocket. "Thanks."

They climbed from the Jeep.

Sienna appeared beside him and looped her arm through his. "Let's go knock 'em dead . . . hubby."

CHAPTER
SIXTEEN

IF JESSE WANTED TO RUN, this would be the perfect time. All he had to do was send a text message or tell Blaine outright what was going on, and Jesse could get out of this whole nightmarish situation.

He was definitely considering that option.

First, he would give this lunch a shot.

But there was no way Blaine or Major Benning was guilty of doing whatever Sienna thought they'd done.

A rush of nerves swept through him as he stepped into the restaurant.

No matter how many years Jesse had worked undercover assignments, he still felt an edge of anxiety sometimes. He told people those nerves kept him sharp—and he really did believe those words were true.

He paused and glanced around the upscale deli. The scent of toasting bread, bubbly cheese, and oven-roasted lunchmeat filled the air until his stomach rumbled. He hadn't realized how hungry he was.

This place wasn't far from Blaine's office. His friend had worked as an accountant after getting out of the military, but Jesse wasn't sure if that's still what Blaine did now.

No sooner had Jesse and Sienna put their names in with the hostess than the door behind them opened again.

Jesse felt a rush of familiarity when he saw Blaine step inside wearing jeans, a polo shirt, and Converse. The woman beside him—she had to be April, his wife—was petite and stylish in an understated type of way.

A grin spread across Jesse's face. "If it isn't my old buddy!"

"Jesse Marx!" Blaine gave him a quick hug.

"Long time no see." Jesse stepped back. "You're looking good, man."

"Thanks. You too." Blaine's gaze fell on Sienna, curiosity glinting in his eyes. "And who is this?"

Sienna extended her hand. "Sienna . . . Sienna *Marx*. Pleasure to meet you."

"You actually managed to talk my friend into settling down?" Blaine raised his eyebrows. "That's quite the accomplishment. I'm impressed."

"I've always liked a challenge." Her eyes glimmered with satisfaction. "Turns out Jesse makes a pretty good partner."

An unexpected surge of delight spread through Jesse.

This is all an act, he reminded himself.

So why did part of him actually like the idea of Sienna being on his arm?

The thought was insane. He needed to have his head examined. Had these people brainwashed him somehow?

He'd set those thoughts aside for later.

"Well, you definitely got a challenge when you married Jesse." Blaine laughed before turning to the woman beside him. "This is my wife, April. Marrying her is the best decision I ever made—no offense to your sister."

Jesse raised his hand, realizing good and well that Blaine and Erica hadn't been a good match. "No offense taken. I'm sorry I couldn't make it to your wedding, but I was on assignment. It's great to meet you, April."

April smiled sweetly. "It's great to meet you also. I've heard a lot about you. All good, of course."

Jesse raised his eyebrow rakishly. "All of it?"

She let out an easy laugh. "Well, *most* of it."

Jesse's lungs already felt looser from the light-hearted, friendly conversation.

Until he remembered his mission.

The last thing he wanted to do was to deceive one of his friends.

He fought a frown.

He'd wait to see how this all played out.

But he wasn't making any promises this would turn out in Sienna's favor.

Sienna thoroughly enjoyed watching Jesse talk to his friends. This was definitely a part of him she hadn't seen or experienced before.

Then again, why would she have?

The two of them were strangers.

Married strangers.

Had Sienna allowed herself to stop long enough to think about that fact, she might have felt a twinge of awkwardness.

But she couldn't go there. It was best if she let herself think of this as an *arrangement*. She and Jesse could figure out all the details later. Even if Jesse walked away without dissolving their marriage, she'd be okay with that.

She liked being alone. Being technically married to Jesse gave her the perfect excuse to ward off any advances from other guys.

Although Sienna didn't need any excuses. She could handle herself on her own, thank you very much.

But, unfortunately, she and Jesse weren't here just to catch up on the good old times.

She needed to think of a way to bring up the subject of Blaine's uncle before this lunch date ended.

As "Honesty" by Billy Joel crooned over speakers in the corner, she swallowed a bite of her Reuben and wiped her mouth. "So, do I understand correctly that your uncle is in the army? That he has a pretty interesting story?"

Blaine nodded. "I guess you managed to get Jesse to open up. Good for you. But, yes, my uncle—Major Roger Benning—became pretty well-known while he was in the army. He was the one who tried to push Benjamin Soldier out of the way when the gunfire erupted. My uncle suffered a couple of bullet wounds, but unfortunately Benjamin passed away despite his efforts."

Jesse's eyes narrowed at the information, and Sienna saw him processing that tidbit.

Benjamin Soldier had been a professional football player who'd given up his career in order to enlist in the army and fight overseas. A terrorist bombing at a hotel in Florida had killed his mother, inspiring him to give up a seven-figure income in order to serve his country.

Unfortunately, after only six months of serving, enemy fire had claimed his life.

He'd become somewhat of an American icon after that.

"What a story," Sienna said. "Your uncle sounds like an honorable man."

"He's a great man. One of my role models for sure." Blaine took another spoonful of his baked potato soup.

"I've always been fascinated with what happened with Benjamin Soldier," Sienna continued. "I mean, I guess most of America would say the same."

"Benjamin Soldier was practically a rock star on the battlefield, and the press *loved* him. For a while, he was one of the best things to happen to the military. They got some great press because of him." Blaine's face fell with remorse. "I still can't believe that he was killed."

"It was definitely an American tragedy," Sienna agreed as she wiped a blob of Thousand Island dressing from her fingers.

"You never met him yourself, did you?" Jesse pushed his empty plate away.

"No, I never met him," Blaine said. "I only heard about him. Sounds like he was a great guy who was taken from us entirely too soon."

Jesse shifted in his seat. "Speaking of the major . . . he lives nearby, doesn't he?"

"As a matter of fact, he does."

"Blaine and I are actually staying at his place." April squeezed Blaine's hand and cast him a smile. "We're still trying to get our new business off the ground, and we need to save some money. So, when Blaine's uncle offered to let us live with him, it seemed like a win-win."

"That's great," Jesse said. "Major Benning is a remarkable man—a true hero. I've always enjoyed talking to him."

"I agree that he's remarkable." Blaine tore off a piece of bread that had been served with his soup. "You should stop by while you're in town. I'm sure he'd love to see you again."

"Thanks for the offer, but we couldn't possibly impose," Jesse said.

Sienna squeezed his arm. "Are you sure? I mean, this sounds like the perfect opportunity."

This was just the opening they were looking for

and the fastest way to find the information they needed.

She waited to hear what Jesse had to say, praying he didn't turn on her now.

CHAPTER
SEVENTEEN

JESSE HAD all kinds of reservations about this conversation. At first, he'd played around with the idea of running, but now this mission was getting too real for him.

Did whatever information Sienna wanted have something to do with Benjamin Soldier? Or did this entirely surround Major Benning?

He had so many questions, questions he couldn't ask right now without raising suspicions.

His thoughts returned to the present, and he realized Blaine was waiting for his response.

"I suppose we could stop by," Jesse finally answered.

"That would be great." Blaine's gaze lit with interest. "My uncle always talks about that time you jumped off the roof and into his pool. He did *not* think it was funny at the time."

"Looking back, it wasn't one of my brightest moves." Jesse shrugged. "Thankfully, everything worked out okay."

As Jesse said the statement, he glanced across the restaurant.

A woman with long hair, stylishly dark at the roots and blonde at the tips—what had his sister called it? Balayage?—sat at the bar wearing a leather jacket and sunglasses.

Jesse couldn't be certain, but he thought she was watching them.

Had this woman been planted here by Sienna? By Blaine?

Or maybe even by the cartel?

She didn't look like anyone he'd ever seen who was associated with the Campeche Cartel, but he wouldn't put anything past the group. Women played powerful roles in the organization, and not all of them were Mexican. They had blended nationalities, which only made it harder to profile their people.

Jesse had been so close to bringing them down—until he'd been discovered. He fought a grimace at the thought.

"I look forward to your visit." Blaine's voice

pulled him back to the present. "What do you say you come by about seven o'clock tonight? Is that too late?"

"We're planning on staying at a hotel about an hour from here." Sienna glanced at Jesse. "Would that put us getting back too late? Jesse hasn't been sleeping well, and late-night driving has been harder because of it."

"Then you should just spend the night." April's eyes lit at the idea. "We have a guesthouse, so why pay for a hotel?"

"Are you sure?" Sienna tilted her head in an earnest look.

"We're sure," Blaine said. "It would be great to catch up."

Jesse smiled. "Then that sounds perfect."

He glanced back at the woman at the bar.

She was gone.

His heart beat harder.

Jesse had no idea what kind of plan he'd just unleashed.

He prayed the outcome wouldn't hurt anyone he cared about.

Sienna's pulse continued to race.

They'd done it.

Not only were they going to get to meet Major Roger Benning, but she and Jesse were going to go to his house to spend the night.

Things couldn't have worked out any better.

"I hate to cut this short." Blaine glanced at the time on his phone. "But since we'll see each other again tonight, that makes it easier. Unfortunately, I have a meeting with an investor that I need to prepare for. But I'm really glad that you called."

Jesse rose also. "It's great to see you again."

No one else could probably see it, but Sienna noticed the strain of guilt in Jesse's voice.

Regret swelled inside her.

She knew she'd asked him to do something hard. But this assignment was important. She wouldn't have gone through all this trouble otherwise.

A few minutes later, their bill was paid, and they stepped out onto the sizzling sidewalk of Phoenix.

Sienna turned to Jesse after his friends left. "You did great."

He scowled as they paused on the sidewalk. "I don't feel great. I feel like a backstabber."

Familiar regret filled her again. "I know. And I wish that wasn't the case."

"What's done is done." Jesse let out a long breath and glanced across the way.

Then he froze.

"What is it?" Sienna asked.

He nodded across the street and down a block. "I think that guy's watching us."

Slowly, Sienna turned, not wanting to be too obvious.

But Jesse was right.

A man stood there. Even though he wore sunglasses, her instincts screamed that they were being watched.

But who would be watching them right now? Who had even known they were going to be here?

Jesse stepped closer and lowered his voice. "Is that one of your guys?"

"What? No. I don't recognize him."

"I saw another woman in the deli. She was watching us. I'm sure of it. Someone clearly knows we're here and wants to send a message. Do you think someone was tipped off that we were coming here today?"

She shook her head. "There's no way anyone could have been tipped off. Monroe and I were very, very careful. We don't tip people off."

"I doubt they're following me since I've been off grid."

Suddenly, her breath caught. "Maybe when we

turned your phone back on, someone was tracking it and got a signal again."

His jaw tightened as realization seemed to wash over him. "I don't like the sound of this."

Sienna glanced back again and saw that the man had started walking toward them.

Her breath caught. "We need to get moving. Now."

Before Jesse could argue, she grabbed his hand, and they hurried down the sidewalk.

CHAPTER
EIGHTEEN

JESSE'S THOUGHTS RUSHED.

Had the cartel tracked him here?

He wouldn't put it past them.

If they had any idea Jesse was still alive, they'd want to finish what they started.

He and Sienna hurried down the sidewalk, not wanting to make too much of a scene.

Not yet, at least.

But if push came to shove, they'd do whatever they needed to do to stay alive.

Jesse glanced over his shoulder again and saw the man had started to jog.

Two other men appeared, forming a web around them.

As Jesse glanced ahead, he spotted another man.

He pulled Sienna to a stop, knowing they needed to regroup.

"They're trying to surround us," he muttered. "Come on."

They took off in a run in the opposite direction. As they darted around a corner, he pulled the phone from his pocket and tossed it into the back of a passing truck.

Maybe that would throw these guys off their trail . . . for a few minutes, at least.

Jesse pulled Sienna inside a nearby office building.

They didn't have much time, so they needed to think quickly.

Without stopping, he rushed to a stairwell and began climbing. Not wanting to get trapped on the roof again, he stopped on the third floor and burst through the fire door into a hallway.

The building seemed to be comprised of several different businesses, all with their own entrances. A dentist's office, a dermatologist, and an advertising company.

"Where are we going?" Sienna glanced down the hallway.

"Somewhere safe, I hope." Jesse pulled her forward.

He glanced at the door on his left and tried the

handle.

It was unlocked.

He and Sienna darted into the small citrus- and pine-scented room.

A janitor's closet, he realized.

Quickly, he shut the door behind them and twisted the lock. He fumbled around in the dark and found what felt like a mop and wedged the handle against the knob.

Their pursuers had to be close. But with any luck, these guys wouldn't know what floor they were on. He and Sienna hadn't had much time to find a place to hide—but he hoped this plan worked.

If not, getting out of here would be tricky.

Jesse would worry about that later.

Right now, he and Sienna just needed to remain hidden.

———

Sienna's heart pounded in her ears at a steady, rapid pace.

Jesse pressed himself against the door, along with something he'd shoved against the handle. Maybe it was a broom or a mop of some sort.

Sienna couldn't tell. She only hoped it held up.

She stood close, ready to act if someone managed to open the door.

She didn't think these guys would easily figure out what floor they were on. She and Jesse could have gone into any of these offices—there were at least six on this floor.

Sienna couldn't be certain, but she thought this whole building was about eight stories.

For now, they just needed to stay quiet.

As everything went still around them, she realized she was standing entirely too close to Jesse.

Her chest was pressed against his arm. Her shoulder against the door.

But she couldn't bring herself to move away.

The scent of his leather jacket drifted toward her as well as the evergreen of his shampoo.

She liked the aromas a little too much.

She glanced behind her, but she could hardly see anything. It was too dark in here.

Sienna had been in life-threatening situations before. Plenty of them. But right now, all her nerves were on edge.

If these guys were the cartel . . . they were ruthless. They wouldn't give up easily.

She had her pistol tucked into a leg holster.

But there had been at least five guys. Even if she

was able to draw and shoot, she and Jesse were still too outnumbered to win.

"It's going to be okay," Jesse murmured.

Something about his reassuring tone made her heart rate slow.

He actually sounded like he believed those words.

Sienna realized she was gripping his arm and loosened her hold. What kind of former CIA operative clung to someone when they were scared?

But all her glib comments were a thing of the past at this very moment.

"Where did they go?" a voice said on the other side of the doorway.

Sienna's breath caught again, and she waited.

"We need to check this hallway. Check *every* hallway."

It was one of the men who'd been chasing them.

They were here.

Close.

Sienna wasn't sure how she and Jesse would get out of the situation alive.

CHAPTER
NINETEEN

JESSE KNEW EXACTLY what they were facing right now.

Trouble.

These guys were cold-blooded.

All they wanted was to kill him.

Since Sienna was with him, by default they'd want to kill her also.

The mop he'd wedged by the door would slow them down some, as well as his body weight that pressed into the door.

But that was really just delaying the inevitable.

If those guys wanted to get in here, they would.

He hadn't brought his gun. In fact, what had happened to his weapon?

Had he had it on the roof when he fell?

He didn't think so.

Maybe it was in his apartment. Or his old car.

There were so many uncertainties right now.

All he knew for sure is he didn't have it now when he needed it most.

He could use the cleaning supplies as a last resort. No doubt there were some corrosive substances that he could spray into someone's eyes.

Which again would slow them down.

Cleaning supplies up against loaded weapons?

There wouldn't be much of a fight.

The best thing Jesse could hope for was that they wouldn't be discovered.

He could feel Sienna leaning into him. Hear her breathing. Smell her sweet perfume.

Sweet? He'd halfway expected her to have the scent of a diva.

But he was getting mixed messages about who she was. Who she *really* was.

Was she a sarcastic, free-spirited CIA operative who'd forced him into marriage?

Or was there more to her, just as Monroe had hinted?

Jesse wasn't sure. Right now wasn't the time to figure it out.

He heard people right outside in the hallway.

Heard other doors opening.

He wished he had a team to help him. Someone to tell him exactly where these guys were and what they were doing.

Just as that thought went through his head, he heard the door handle to the closet rattle.

It looked like he and Sienna were out of time.

Sienna reached down and grabbed the gun from her holster. She grasped it, ready to use it if necessary.

She'd gotten Jesse into this.

As soon as someone burst through this door, she would push Jesse behind her and would take whatever bullets she could. Maybe buy him some time or give him a fighting chance to get away.

Based on what she heard outside the door, only two people were in this hallway.

These guys had probably split up to look for them.

That would make this a little easier.

But her muscles tightened as she waited.

She heard the door handle rattle again.

"Marco thinks he found them," one of the guys said outside the door. "They escaped out the back. Come on."

Footsteps thundered away.

Then silence stretched.

Were those guys really gone? Or was this just a ruse?

Sienna didn't dare release the breath she held in her lungs.

She and Jesse needed to be certain before they moved.

Finally, after a minute passed, Jesse turned to her. "Do you think they're gone?"

"It seems like it. Let me peek my head out to be sure."

Jesse touched her shoulder. "I can do that."

Sienna wasn't much into chauvinistic behavior. But she decided this time just to let Jesse. She needed to save her energy for what was important.

Still, she held her breath as he quietly cracked the door open and peered out.

She prayed there wasn't trouble waiting for them.

But she also knew that they weren't in the clear yet.

They were either going to have to figure out how to get back to the Jeep without being spotted or they'd have to find a new vehicle.

There was a good chance these guys had already staked out the Jeep she and Jesse had left in the parking garage.

No, their troubles were just beginning.

They didn't have time to deal with this right now.

Having members of the cartel find Jesse had not been on Sienna's schedule for today.

CHAPTER
TWENTY

JESSE TOOK Sienna's hand as he crept from the closet.

These guys could still be close.

That meant he and Sienna needed to be very careful.

From his memory, one door to this building was located at the front, where he and Sienna had run inside. He'd also seen a matching door on the opposite side of the building.

But, certainly, a building of this size had more than two exits.

He just needed to figure out where they were—especially since he couldn't be certain of these guys' location.

He slipped his leather jacket off and handed it to Sienna. "Put this on."

She stared at him a moment before complying. In other circumstances, he might feign shock. But not right now.

As he walked past a coat rack outside a dentist office, Jesse grabbed an old sweatshirt that had been left there and slipped it on. The change of clothing would help disguise him and hopefully buy them some time.

Without any prompting, Sienna pulled her hair into a bun and slipped some sunglasses on.

The changes were subtle, but they could throw someone off their trail . . . for a few minutes, at least.

A few minutes might be all they needed to get out of here.

They rushed to the stairway and hurried to the first floor.

Jesse peered out the fire door, saw the coast was clear, and then stepped into the hallway with Sienna.

A deli located at the edge of the lobby caught his eye.

That was where they needed to go.

Acting as if they belonged in this building, Jesse and Sienna strolled behind the deli counter and into the kitchen.

The guy behind the counter noticed them just as they slipped inside and yelled, "Hey!"

The two of them kept running until they reached a door leading to an alley out back.

Stepping outside, Jesse quickly surveyed the area to see if any of those guys were back there.

He saw no one.

Sienna paused beside him, her cheeks looking flushed with adrenaline as she also surveyed the area.

"We can't go back to the Jeep," Sienna said. "These guys probably have it staked out."

Jesse's lips flickered down in a frown as his body remained poised for action. "I agree. These guys will keep looking until they find us. You know that, don't you?"

"Now I do. I should have never given you that phone back." Her jaw tightened as she shook her head. "It was a rookie mistake."

"Don't beat yourself up over it. You were just trying to earn my trust. What do you think we should do?" Jesse knew Sienna had experience with this kind of thing also. For a long time, he'd been a lone ranger in his undercover work, but he still believed in the power of teamwork.

They paused beside a dumpster, still on alert as they glanced around.

"We can go out there and blend in," Sienna said.

"But I think the best thing we can do right now is find somewhere to lie low and bide our time."

His thoughts raced before stopping at one idea. "I think I might have just the place we can go. Come with me."

Still holding hands, Jesse pulled Sienna toward the sidewalk. They darted across the busy street cutting through the downtown high rises and ducked into another alley. They kept weaving between buildings until they reached a park on the edge of town.

Once there, Jesse paused behind a tree and glanced around.

He didn't see anyone.

"We'll be safe here for a little while," he murmured. "But we still need to remain on guard."

Sienna glanced around also, double-checking his assessment—just as he would expect her to do. "Absolutely."

He drank in a deep breath, knowing he had to remain vigilant.

Sienna stared up at him and released the air from her lungs before murmuring, "Things just got really interesting."

Jesse let out a half grunt/half chuckle. "You can say that again."

"This park is nice." Sienna paced the edge of the park with Jesse, her eyes wide open.

She wished her lungs would loosen up some—as they should being in a beautiful place like this. Even the sun seemed bright and cheery—and not too hot.

She'd like to relax. To enjoy the moment. But that wouldn't be wise. She needed to remain on guard.

Those guys had found them once.

There was a good chance they'd be able to find them again.

At least Jesse didn't have his phone on him any longer.

Jesse glanced around at the park again with its manmade stream, sculptures, and paved walkways. "I've always liked it here."

She looked at him curiously, wondering about his statement. "So, you've been here before?"

"I grew up in Texas, but when my parents divorced when I was twelve, my father moved here," Jesse explained. "He died a few years back."

"I'm sorry to hear that."

"I haven't been back since the funeral. My stepmom still lives here, but we weren't close. She has her own children anyway." Jesse slowed his steps. "But back when I used to visit my dad, I came here to hang out a few times. Honestly, I met a girl, and this was her favorite park. That's the main reason I know about this place."

"A girlfriend, huh?" Curiosity gleamed in her gaze.

"She was the one bright spot about coming to Phoenix. But we only dated a few months, and I realized it wasn't going to work out."

"At least, you got to visit your dad."

"What I really wanted was for my mom and dad to get back together. But that wasn't going to happen. So, I learned to adjust, I suppose."

"Sometimes that's all we can do, right?"

"Absolutely."

They began walking again—but looking over their shoulders with every step. Those guys could appear at any minute. But the two of them also needed to blend in. Running and acting frantic would only draw more attention to them.

"Where did you grow up?" Jesse asked.

"Alabama," she said. "Near Gulf Shores."

"That's a nice area."

She glanced at him in surprise. "You've been there?"

"As a matter of fact, yes, I have. I went there with some buddies of mine back when we were on leave one time."

"I can only imagine the trouble you guys got yourselves into."

"What happens in Gulf Shores stays in Gulf Shores!" He grinned, his eyes twinkling. "That was back when I was young and stupid. I'd like to think I've grown up since then, developed some stronger standards."

He was an interesting guy—and not as macho as Sienna had assumed.

He glanced at her as they continued strolling. "You seem to be right at home at the ranch."

She nodded and slowed her gait. "I am. I love it there, far more than I thought I would."

"Why did you get out of government work?"

Her words caught in her throat. She didn't want to go there. Didn't want to dive into this with him.

Before she could respond, someone ducked behind a tree just ahead.

Those guys had found them, she realized.

Now she and Jesse had to decide: fight or flight.

CHAPTER
TWENTY-ONE

"JESSE! WATCH OUT!"

He turned in time to see a man charging at them —with a gun drawn.

Several people nearby screamed before scattering.

Hopefully, that meant there wouldn't be any collateral damage if this guy started shooting.

"You don't want to do this." Sienna had her hands fisted in front of her.

"Move out of the way, lady. Our beef isn't with you."

Jesse stared at the man. He'd never seen him before.

But he was certain this guy was a member of the Campeche Cartel.

"You can leave, Sienna," Jesse murmured. "He's right. This isn't about you."

"No way I'm leaving my husband to fight on his own."

Jesse might smile—in different circumstances. He knew he wouldn't talk Sienna out of this, and he didn't want to waste his energy trying. Besides, with his injuries, he wasn't at the top of his game right now. Having capable backup was a good idea.

"Your husband?" the man repeated, his eyebrows knotting together.

At his words, Sienna swung her leg in a round-house kick. Her foot hit his gun, knocking it out of his hands.

Jesse lunged for it and grabbed it as the man took off in a run.

Sienna took a step forward but stopped. "Should we go after him?"

Jesse's jaw tightened as he watched the man disappear. "It won't do any good. He's just one of many players. Knowing our luck, that guy will just lead us right back into his web."

That was how these guys worked . . . and they couldn't risk that.

An hour later, Jesse and Sienna headed down the road in the Jeep. To his surprise, Sienna had asked him if he wanted to drive—if he felt up to it.

Since he hadn't taken any pain meds, he'd agreed.

They'd already checked the vehicle over for any tracking devices, but they found none.

They'd asked a valet who'd just gotten off duty to bring the Jeep out of the garage for them. After slipping him fifty bucks, the guy had agreed.

Their plan seemed to have worked. They'd gotten the Jeep back. No one had confronted the valet, and Jesse and Sienna hadn't spotted anyone following them.

Jesse had to admit he found a small sense of satisfaction in being back in the game, back in the middle of an investigation.

He loved being out in the field. Something about it got his blood racing.

But Jesse had two separate issues at the moment: the vengeance-seeking cartel and Sienna, who clearly had some type of ulterior motive.

He wanted to trust the woman. He really did.

But that wouldn't be wise. Not yet. There were still too many unknowns.

She typed something into her phone before pointing to the street up ahead. "Turn here."

"You memorized the address?"

"Of course. What kind of operative would I be if I didn't?"

"Enough said." He didn't want to be impressed by the woman, but he'd be lying if he said he wasn't.

They headed away from downtown Phoenix into a more residential area with rolling hills surrounding it.

"Beautiful area," Sienna muttered.

"It is—and it's also incredibly hot in the summer."

A few minutes later, he and Sienna pulled up to a sprawling Santa Fe-style home with stucco siding, elegant landscape lighting, and a terra-cotta roof. The sun was beginning to set behind the hills in the distance, creating a picture-perfect image.

"Nice house," Sienna muttered as she leaned forward to stare at it.

"Yes, it is. My impression is that Major Benning stays here on the weekends and up at Camp Navajo near Flagstaff during the week."

"I'm glad our timing worked out."

Their conversation sounded so casual—but it felt anything but.

He parked the Jeep and turned toward Sienna. "Do you really think he has something to do with those deaths you mentioned?"

She stared at the house still. "He's connected with

all three people who died. I'm not saying he's behind their murders. But he might be able to help us figure out some answers—as soon as we know we can trust him."

He felt much more comfortable with that explanation—yet still in no hurry to get this plan underway.

"That's a pretty cool story with him and Benjamin Soldier, isn't it?" he said instead.

Sienna offered a tight smile. "Yes, it most certainly is."

Before getting out of the Jeep, Jesse lifted a prayer for wisdom.

He wasn't sure he knew what he was doing—and that wasn't something he often said.

Making the situation worse . . . he had no idea at this point who he could trust.

Not his friends.

Not his colleagues.

And definitely not his new wife.

SIENNA SMOOTHED HER DRESS, determined to look like a faithful wife and a good friend.

And not like a former CIA operative on a mission.

If anything, today had served to form a bond between her and Jesse. This time when they held hands as they walked into the house, it didn't feel quite as strange or foreign.

In fact, maybe part of Sienna was starting to like the friendship they were forging a little more than she should.

Blaine and April greeted them at the door with wide grins.

To anyone watching, this would seem like a normal get-together between friends. But Sienna knew that it was anything but. Even though she'd lived a life of subterfuge, part of her hated the deceit. How things were never simple.

That's why she liked the ranch so much.

Even though the lives of the people they helped were complicated, somehow everything seemed easier—more cut and dried. Best part of it all, she could simply be herself.

"My uncle's just finishing up a phone call, but he'll be out here to join us soon." Blaine stepped back. "Come on inside."

The interior of the home was just as lovely as the outside, with terra-cotta floors and plants decorating various surfaces. Sienna commented on how lovely it was.

Somewhere in the distance, she smelled fish and spicy peppers and maybe even some cumin.

"Why don't you have a seat and we'll get you something to drink?" April led them to a glass-top table decorated with fresh flowers.

As Blaine got them drinks, April filled them in on the startup company they were working to get off the ground. Apparently, April was a fitness influencer when Blaine had met her. Together, they were trying to launch a company that would allow personal trainers to come to people's homes while tracking everything via an app.

Sienna smiled politely and asked all the right

questions. But what she really wanted was to meet the major. To dig more into his life. To figure out what he knew—or what he might be hiding.

Finally, twenty minutes after they arrived, Major Benning stepped out.

Sienna straightened her spine as she readied herself to ensure her mission would be successful.

Jesse rose to his feet as the familiar figure entered the room. "Major."

Major Benning grinned as he stepped closer. "Jesse Marx . . . it's been a long time. You were a mere boy last time I saw you."

"You were young last time I saw you too."

The major chuckled. "I suppose I deserved that. Good to see you, my boy."

Jesse observed the man a moment. Five foot ten and thin, his salt-and-pepper hair was only present around the edge of his head and on his upper lip. He carried himself upright like someone who'd spent a lifetime in the military.

His gaze fell on Sienna. "And who is this beauty?"

Jesse introduced her as his wife.

Curiosity flickered in the major's eyes. "Let's

have a seat and talk," he said. "Dolores will be serving our food tonight. She's my part-time cook and housecleaner. She's been my saving grace since Vivian died two years ago."

"I was so sorry to hear about her car accident," Jesse said as he sat down again. "She was a good woman."

"Yes, she was." His gaze turned back to Sienna. "Now, tell me . . . how did the two of you meet?"

Jesse glanced at Sienna. The two of them had been through their cover story several times. But now they had to not only recite it but sell it.

He slipped his arm around the back of her chair. "We were actually parachuting at the time. We were in the same group, but we didn't know each other. I ran into a little trouble."

"His chute malfunctioned," Sienna quickly added. "It didn't deploy."

"What?" The major's eyes widened.

"I saw it all happen." Sienna continued. "My instructor and I were able to grab Jesse and safely land him."

"And I had to buy her dinner afterward—just to say thank you." He grinned at her, making sure the motion looked sickly sweet.

"What about the instructor?" Blaine asked.

"He just got a thank you." Jesse let out a laugh. "I

knew I couldn't let Sienna walk away without getting to know her more. I had to give it a shot, or I knew I'd regret it." He glanced at Sienna, his gaze softening. "It was love at first sight, wasn't it, sweetie?"

"You can say that again. We were married only a week later."

The major's eyebrows shot up. "That quickly?"

Jesse shrugged. "When you know, you know."

"I guess so!"

A woman entered with plates of food. "Dinner is served!"

As steaming dishes of fish tacos, Spanish rice, beans, and guacamole were served, everyone dug in.

But Jesse knew the conversation couldn't stay this casual for long.

They needed to get down to business soon—before all their time was gone.

CHAPTER
TWENTY-THREE

SIENNA TRIED to ignore the feeling of Jesse's arm around her and how natural the motion felt.

They were on a job, and she needed to keep reminding herself of that fact.

She stabbed a cucumber with her fork and turned to the major. "So, I hear that you've had quite the career."

He smiled. "That depends on who you ask. Certainly, not some of the soldiers who I made run until they passed out. Needless to say, they weren't cut out for my line of work. But there were many good men and women who proved to be exemplary soldiers."

"Blaine and April were telling me that you actually knew Benjamin Soldier," Sienna started, trying to sound casual. "That's really remarkable. I've been fascinated by his story for a long time."

"Benjamin was a great guy. One of the best. Very noble and honorable." The major frowned and rubbed his jaw as memories seemed to fill his gaze. "He was taken from us entirely too soon. I wish I could have prevented his death. I did what I could . . ."

Jesse shifted in his seat, his gaze softening. "It's admirable that you tried to throw him out of the way like you did."

"The men in my squadron were important to me. I would have given my life for any of them. I'm just sorry that it wasn't possible to save Benjamin."

"I'm sure an incident like that bonded all of you," Jesse added.

"It did. For the longest time, we all stayed in touch. But, sometimes, I feel as if that squadron was cursed."

Sienna tilted her head. "What do you mean?"

"There were eight of us altogether on a mission in the Middle East. Now, only four of us are left. That reality is quite sobering."

"Most of the squadron would be in their forties now, right?" Sienna continued. "That seems like you guys are awfully young to have lost so many. Unless they were lost on the battlefield."

Major Benning's gaze instantly sharpened. "No, they were all stateside when they died. I've attended three funerals in the past six months. That actually seems surreal."

"I'm sorry," Sienna said. "That sounds terrible. What happened to them?"

"It has been difficult. One died of a heart attack. Another in an auto accident. And another because of a home invasion that turned deadly."

Sienna's throat tightened when she heard the grief in the major's voice. "The timing on that . . . it's strange, isn't it?"

The major raised his eyebrows. "You can say that again."

Jesse listened carefully. The major definitely didn't seem as if he'd had a part in what was going on. In fact, he seemed to be mourning.

What exactly were they supposed to find out here?

"Enough of this sad subject," the major said. "Let's talk about happier things."

Jesse realized that their opportunity may have slipped away. But he could understand the subject change.

For the next two hours, they reminisced. Talked about military life. Talked about mutual friends.

It wasn't what Sienna wanted. Jesse knew that. But the change was nice.

Dolores served berry trifle and decaf coffee on the patio before departing for the evening.

"By the way, why did you say you were in the area again?" The major turned to Jesse.

"I've taken some time off work to travel and do some honeymooning." Jesse smiled at Sienna. "Working undercover started to take its toll on me. It's been good to get away, to try to relax some."

"Rest is good for the soul." Before the major could say anything else, his phone buzzed.

He glanced at the screen and frowned before typing something there.

As he put his phone down, his gaze looked clouded.

"Is everything okay?" Blaine asked.

"Of course," he said. "It's just a work thing."

But Jesse had to wonder if there was more to it.

CHAPTER
TWENTY-FOUR

THE MAJOR KNEW MORE than he was letting on. Sienna was sure of it.

The man was friendly on the outside. But she had been trained to read people. To recognize telltale signs.

He was hiding something.

What exactly had the text he'd just received been about?

She needed to figure out a way to find out.

She saw her opportunity when he excused himself to run inside to the bathroom.

He'd left his phone on the table. Now she just needed to figure out a way to look at the screen without anyone asking any questions.

As the seconds ticked past, she waited for her opportunity. She knew she didn't have much time.

Glancing around, she looked for something that could distract people before the major returned.

As Jesse, Blaine, and April got caught up in another conversation about their startup, she found a small rock on the ground. When they weren't looking, she tossed it across the yard.

It hit a fountain in the distance, and everyone turned toward the sound.

"What was that?" Jesse's shoulders visibly bristled.

"Probably just a bird." Blaine rose to his feet. "I suppose I should check it out just to make sure."

Sienna held her breath as she watched, hoping that her plan had worked.

Sure enough, all three of them rose to see what had caused the noise.

"I'm just going to finish my coffee," she said.

But as soon as their backs were toward her, she tapped the major's phone.

The screen lit.

She knew she didn't have time to get into his device and dig around.

But she saw three snippets of text messages on the lock screen, and she hoped that one of them might be revealing.

One was a weather forecast for the next day.

The next was a breaking news update about something happening overseas.

But the third was from a man named Ted Colins.

She quickly read the words there.

If you know what's smart, you'll do what I say.

That did *not* sound friendly.

She started to reach for the phone, desperate to know more.

But before she could, the patio door slid open again, and the major stepped out.

The rest of the group also joined them.

Sienna's mind raced.

She stored that name away at the back of her mind. Ted Colins.

He was worth looking into.

After dessert, April led Jesse and Sienna to a guesthouse located beside a large, turquoise-lined pool with multiple waterfalls and a hot tub. Lights in the pool changed color, alternating from pink to purple to green.

Stars twinkled in the dark sky, and palm trees towered over them.

April pushed open the door to the guesthouse. "You guys can stay here. It's pretty simple, but I think you'll be comfortable. This is one of the major's favorite places. He escapes out here to 'think about life,' as he says. I hope you both will like it as well."

Jesse glanced around the small, clean space before flashing a smile. "This looks perfect. Thank you so much for your hospitality."

"Of course. The fridge is fully stocked, or you're welcome to join us for breakfast in the morning. I'm sure the major won't mind."

"We just may do that, but I know we also need to head back fairly early." Sienna stepped closer to Jesse and wrapped her arm around his waist. "But thank you so much for your generosity in letting us stay here. This is so much better than a hotel."

April grinned. "I'm so glad you like it. I hope you have a good night—and feel free to use the pool if you'd like. There are a couple of extra bathing suits in the dresser."

As soon as April closed the door, Sienna released Jesse and stepped back. They turned to each other, and a moment of awkwardness stretched between them.

Staying together in the same room was *definitely* not what either of them had in mind.

Jesse had hoped when he heard the word "guest-house" that there would be more than one bedroom, which would make this easier. Instead, the space had an open layout with a bed in the corner, a small kitchenette, a bathroom, and a small couch.

"This will be cozy." Sienna glanced around and shook her head.

"That's one way to put it." Jesse turned to her. "Before we figure out the sleeping situation, what did you think of the conversation tonight?"

"I think we need to talk to Ted Colins."

"Who?"

"The major got a text from him during dessert. It said: If you know what's smart, you'll do what I say."

"Sounds threatening."

"Exactly." Sienna nodded. "Maybe this guy knows something."

"He's definitely worth looking into."

CHAPTER
TWENTY-FIVE

AS SIENNA'S statement hung in the air, Jesse snapped from his stupor. He wasn't going to figure out these motives by just standing here.

Instead, he nodded toward the sofa. "I'll take the couch tonight."

"Don't be ridiculous. You're injured, and you're way too tall to sleep there."

He sliced his hand through the air. "Injury or not, I was raised to be a gentleman. There's no way I'm going to let you take the couch."

Sienna stared at him as if contemplating her options. Finally, she nodded. "Fine. Have it your way. But don't say I didn't offer."

Jesse grabbed an extra pillow and found a blanket in the drawer. He tossed them both on the couch, dreading sleeping there. His legs would have to be propped on the armrest at the end.

But the arrangement would work. He'd certainly slept in worse situations.

Sienna slipped into the bathroom and emerged a moment later wearing shorts and a T-shirt.

Jesse dragged his gaze away from her.

That woman looked good in whatever she wore. A dress. A cowgirl outfit. Or slouchy shorts and a T-shirt.

The more he got to know Sienna, the more fascinated he was by her.

But if he was smart, he'd kill that fascination before it went any further.

Instead, he removed his shoes, lay back on the couch, and pulled the blanket over him, trying to relax. He stared at the ceiling, at a decorative tile there that was crooked, and stopped himself from straightening it.

Sienna climbed into bed and propped herself up against the headboard, letting out a sigh before flipping off the light on the nightstand beside her.

Subtle darkness fell over the room, though a glow from an outside light crept through the windows.

Jesse settled in, praying he'd be able to get some rest.

"I can't sleep."

Sienna blinked as she pressed her head into the pillow.

Had Jesse just said he couldn't sleep?

She pushed herself up in bed, glad she wasn't the only one. "I can't either. I have too much on my mind."

She glanced across the room and saw him sitting up on the couch, his hair rumpled and a blanket around his waist.

"Any desire to go for a swim?" he asked.

A moment of panic raced through her at the thought of wearing a bathing suit. There was a time in her life when she wouldn't have thought twice about it.

But not after Munich. Not after Todd.

"I'm not much of a swimming pool girl," she finally said.

"Maybe it would be good for us both to cool off and relax a moment."

"I don't know . . . maybe I could dangle my feet in." That seemed like a safe compromise.

Even across the dim room, Sienna saw Jesse squint in confusion. She couldn't blame him. She wasn't normally timid.

"You don't seem like a dangle your feet type of girl," he finally said.

Sienna shrugged as she tried to play it off. "I don't have a bathing suit. I know April said there were some extra ones, but I'd be content just to sit on the edge."

"Then so be it. Let's go for it."

Dread welled inside her.

Sienna hadn't expected the reaction. But it was there. Scars from the past—both physical and emotional—had proven to be more powerful in her life than she'd thought. And as much as she wanted to believe that she didn't care what Jesse Marx thought about her, she knew she did.

The scar across her chest seemed to throb at the thought.

Jesse disappeared into the bathroom and emerged a moment later in a swimsuit that seemed to fit him just right. He tossed her a towel before they both stepped outside toward the pool.

Wasting no time, Jesse dove right in.

Sienna couldn't help but smile as she watched him glide through the water, almost as if his cracked ribs were a thing of the past.

She placed her towel on the pavers and made herself comfortable on the edge of the pool with her feet dangling in the cool water.

A moment later, Jesse surfaced in front of her, water dripping down his face as he stared up at her. "You sure you don't want to get in? It feels great."

"I'm positive." She was tempted. The old Sienna would have dived right in. But things had changed—things she had no control over.

Jesse stared at her another moment, and Sienna knew he was confused—and curious.

She didn't blame him.

Very few things held her back from doing what she wanted. Everyone had always told her she was fearless and brazen.

And, in most areas of her life, Sienna was.

But having nearly lost her life after being stabbed—to the point where she'd had several heart surgeries that left a hideous scar across her chest—had brought out her insecurities. Even with time, she still didn't feel comfortable wearing a bathing suit.

She didn't know Jesse well enough to tell him that.

It was too personal.

Too private.

The memories too painful.

"Have it your way." Jesse turned and dove back into the water.

She smiled.

The man was different than she'd thought he'd be —a good kind of different.

In other circumstances, maybe the two of them would even make a good team.

But it was better if Sienna kept her distance. She felt a connection with Jesse—one she didn't want to feel. One that was unexpected and unwelcome.

She should have already put on the brakes and stopped herself from starting to like the man more. She shouldn't have admired his integrity and charm.

She knew better.

Her feelings didn't matter right now. She had to focus on the task at hand. She'd made a promise to Charlie, and she intended to keep it.

CHAPTER
TWENTY-SIX

JESSE HAD BEEN TRYING to read Sienna all evening.

But he was clearly clueless because he had no idea what was going through her head.

Instead, he tried to respect her boundaries and not ask too many questions.

However, she was notably more somber as she sat at the poolside watching him.

He lay on an inflatable chair, floating on the water and almost feeling relaxed, despite the circumstances.

He wanted to get to know her. Wanted to know about her past. How she'd gotten into the CIA. What made her tick. If she had brothers or sisters. What she liked to do in her free time.

But, suddenly, her glib was gone and her walls were up.

Jesse sensed that now wasn't the time to push.

"What do you think about sneaking into the major's house tonight?" she asked after a moment of silence.

His eyebrows shot up. "That's a terrible idea."

"This could be our opportunity."

"If we're caught, then we've just lost our best lead." Jesse said the words as if he was a willing participant in this farce.

"I don't want to miss this opportunity." She shrugged like none of this was a big deal.

"Don't do it." He locked gazes with her. "Promise me you won't."

Sienna stared at him silently a moment before letting out a sigh and nodding. "Okay, fine. I won't."

Relief washed through him.

At least, he could sleep better tonight knowing that. Because until he knew for sure that the major was somehow involved with this, he wasn't going to risk his friendship.

Nothing Sienna said would change his mind.

Sienna had hardly been able to sleep all night.

She'd gotten up several times and paced, trying to burn off energy without waking Jesse.

Maybe she felt so restless because she was all too aware that Jesse snoozed only several feet away.

Every time she thought he was sleeping, she slit her eyes open and studied him.

It wasn't that she hadn't been able to study Jesse before. But now that she knew him better, the man seemed much more interesting.

He'd surprised her.

Sienna had thought he'd be all testosterone and adrenaline. But Jesse had a sensitive side. She'd expected him to keep his walls up and remain cold. But she'd seen something in his gaze yesterday—a real curiosity and a genuine concern.

She wasn't sure why, but the sight of his warm gaze had done something to her heart.

Despite her best efforts, she felt some of the walls she'd put up beginning to crumble.

That was a plot twist she hadn't seen coming.

As the sun came up, she escaped to the bathroom to get ready for the day.

When she emerged, Jesse was awake and sitting on the couch with a sleepy look on his face. "Morning."

She nodded at him. "Good morning. How did you sleep?"

"Not great. But that's to be expected."

Sienna had figured that would be his answer.

She sighed.

Today was a new day with a new task at hand. She didn't want to leave Phoenix without answers. But figuring out her next step wasn't exactly clear.

"What do you say we go inside and have breakfast before we leave?" Jesse asked. "I figure the more we can talk to Blaine and April or even the major, the better."

"I was hoping you might say that," Sienna said. "That sounds perfect."

Jesse folded the blanket and straightened the couch cushions before taking his turn in the bathroom.

When he was ready, they started toward the house.

Halfway there, a scream cut through the air.

Sienna and Jesse glanced at each other before taking off to see what was wrong.

CHAPTER
TWENTY-SEVEN

JESSE SPRINTED TOWARD THE HOUSE, adrenaline pumping through him.

That had to be April's scream he'd heard.

What had happened?

He felt Sienna at his heels. Neither of them eased up until they reached the back of the house. He lunged for the door and twisted the handle.

It was unlocked.

Jesse barged into the house and glanced around, trying to figure out where the scream had come from.

He spotted April emerging from a hallway in the distance. Her face was pale, and her hands were shaky.

He rushed toward her. "What happened? Are you okay?"

She shook her head, her gaze looking glazed and

unsteady. "It's the major . . . he didn't come out for his normal coffee so Blaine went in to check on him. Jesse . . . he's dead."

Jesse felt the blood drain from his face. "What? How? When?"

"I'm not sure. There's no blood or anything. Maybe he just died in his sleep. I don't know. I just can't believe this." She burst into tears.

Sienna wrapped an arm around April's shoulders, murmuring soft words of comfort.

"Did you call 911?" Jesse asked.

"Blaine did. He's in his uncle's room still."

Jesse rushed past them, anxious to see for himself what had happened.

But as he stepped into the major's room, he had one overwhelming thought: what if Sienna had done this?

Fifteen minutes later, the police had shown up and were processing the scene.

Sienna stayed by April, trying to do whatever she could to make the woman feel better, even though she knew there was no real comfort in a situation like this.

Still, she busied herself with helping Dolores get coffee for people, all while offering condolences.

Working in this role had never been Sienna's forte. But she was determined to do whatever she could to help.

On occasion, she noticed Jesse glancing at her from across the room.

But a new look filled his gaze.

The friendliness from last night seemed to have disappeared, and it had been replaced by . . . hostility?

Sienna wasn't sure why. What had she done?

Then all at once, the truth hit her.

Jesse was wondering if she'd killed the major, wasn't he?

It made sense.

She'd been sent here on a mission, and now the major was dead.

The thought stung, more than it should.

How would she convince Jesse that she didn't have anything to do with this?

She wasn't sure she'd be able to—not when all the pieces were in place.

For now, she was simply thankful that Jesse hadn't called her out. That he was remaining cordial —at least in public.

Sienna had a feeling it would be a different story as soon as they were alone.

She resisted the urge to march over to him and set him straight. Now wasn't the time or place.

She let out a sigh and took another shaky sip of her coffee.

The paramedics had arrived shortly after the police, but they hadn't been able to revive the major. She had no doubt the FBI would probably arrive, maybe even USACID—the United States Army Criminal Investigative Division.

Sienna only prayed that Jesse would maintain his cover when the FBI showed up. She hadn't told him he was being investigated. But it seemed she should mention the fact to him before the feds arrived.

What she really wanted to do was run.

But she knew that would only make her look even more guilty.

And looking guilty was the last thing she wanted right now.

CHAPTER
TWENTY-EIGHT

JESSE COULDN'T STOP THINKING about the possibility that Sienna was behind this.

Especially since he'd heard her get out of bed last night and step outside.

Had she disappeared long enough to kill the major?

Was she using Jesse this whole time? Earning his trust so she could do this very thing?

He didn't know, but the more he thought about it, the more turmoil churned inside him.

He didn't want to waste more time.

He wanted to ask her about it.

Now.

To confront her.

But he also knew that might make things worse.

He had to keep his timing in check.

"Jesse . . . there's something you need to know," Sienna whispered as she poured a cup of coffee in the kitchen.

He bristled.

Was she going to admit to what she'd done?

"I don't think I want to know." He glanced around, surveying the house for trouble or listening ears.

"Jesse . . ." She squeezed his arm, her gaze pleading with him.

Before she could say what was on her mind, three more people arrived.

FBI agents.

His spirits lifted when he saw one of his colleagues, Ian Murphy, step inside. He'd worked with him back in San Antonio five years ago. The short, stout man had a Scandinavian heritage and quiet demeanor.

Ian stared at him a moment as recognition flooded his features. "Jesse?"

"Ian. It's me."

Ian shook his hand before glancing around. "I didn't realize you were here."

"I'm only here as a friend," Jesse said. "Blaine and I go way back, and I just happened to be in town last night. My . . ." He glanced at Sienna. "My wife and I were staying in the guesthouse when we heard a scream."

Ian's eyebrows shot up. "Your wife?"

Jesse shrugged. "It's been a while since we've caught up. A few years, at least."

Ian went into professional mode. "I wish we *could* catch up, but I heard what happened. I'm going to need to ask everybody some questions."

Jesse's thoughts raced.

How much should he say?

This was his opportunity to get out of all this and away from Sienna. He'd done as he'd promised. He'd brought her to meet with Blaine. And look what had happened now.

He would need to figure out what he was going to do soon.

But could he leave now knowing what Sienna might have done?

Sienna didn't want to feel nervous.

But as her coffee mug clattered onto the counter-top, it was clear that she was.

Which was unlike her.

She didn't know what bothered her the most.

The fact that Jesse could sell her out to the police.

Or just the mere fact that Jesse was doubting her right now.

She quickly cleaned up the coffee, noticing that some of the dark liquid had gotten on her shirt.

She pointed to the guesthouse. "I'm going to change real quick, but I'll be back."

"I'll walk with you." Jesse suddenly appeared beside her.

A shiver raked through her. "Of course."

Without saying anything else, they stepped outside into the bright sunshine. It wasn't until they were inside the guesthouse that Jesse turned toward her.

He didn't just turn toward her. His muscles bristled as his hands went to his hips, and he practically backed her into a corner.

Accusation stained his gaze. "You did this, didn't you?"

Sienna's heart pounded into her rib cage. "Of course not. I told you I wasn't going to go inside their house, and I didn't."

"Then where did you go last night?"

Her eyebrows shot up. So, he *had* noticed that, hadn't he?

She'd tried to be quiet so she would go unnoticed. She was usually good at being sneaky.

"I went and sat outside by the pool for a little while. I needed to clear my head."

He let out a skeptical grunt. "Because you *love* getting in the pool."

She frowned. "It's complicated."

"You really like saying that, don't you?" His eyes practically shot laser beams into her.

"I don't know what to say to convince you. But I didn't kill the major."

Jesse stepped back and dragged his hand through his hair. "I'm just not sure about that. This seems like the perfect setup to me. You convince me to go along with you on this mission. You make it sound like your intentions are noble. But maybe your intentions this whole time have been to get me to trust you so you could get inside the major's house."

"Jesse . . . you should know me by now. You know that's not true." She heard the almost wounded tone to her voice. The sound surprised her just as much as it might anyone.

Anger flashed in his gaze. "But do I really know you? No. I don't know anything about you other than your name and that you used to be CIA. Every time I think you're going to be real, you clam up again. I feel like I've had the wool pulled over my eyes every time I try to trust you."

Sienna stepped toward him and started to reach

out her hand. But when she saw Jesse bristle, she dropped it back to her side. "It's not like that."

He let out a long breath and glanced beyond her as if gathering his thoughts.

"The major visited each of the three men who died," she announced.

"What?" Disbelief stretched through his voice.

"I didn't want to mention it, but now I can't keep it quiet. We initially suspected he might be behind their deaths. Now, it's clear he wasn't."

"Why would he go visit those men?"

She shrugged. "I have no idea."

Jesse stared into the distance another moment.

"Are you going to tell Special Agent Murphy what's happening?" Sienna's voice sounded strained as it cut through the silence.

"That's what I need to figure out."

Her heart pounded in her ears.

In the old days, Sienna would take steps to ensure that her cover wasn't blown. She'd subdue anyone who threatened her mission.

But she didn't want to go that far with Jesse. She wanted the two of them to have an amicable working relationship.

It was more than that, really. She wanted to be friends with him.

Sienna realized that might sound funny considering the way this had all started.

But something had changed in the process during this trip.

At least, she thought it had.

Now, she didn't know what to expect.

Suddenly the tables had turned. Jesse had the upper hand. He could expose her. Ruin the entire mission.

But would he?

CHAPTER
TWENTY-NINE

JESSE TOOK a step back from Sienna as they faced each other.

He didn't know what to think.

Part of him wanted to trust Sienna.

But how could he? He hardly even knew her.

Yet she seemed earnestly truthful right now.

Then again, she had made her living lying.

She had forced him into marriage.

Essentially, she'd forced him into this assignment.

Jesse wasn't sure why he bothered to trust this woman at all. What had she ever done to earn his trust?

She *had* saved him out in that desert when the man pulled a gun on him. But that had been for her own benefit more than it had been for his. Even though they'd worked well together, that still didn't mean anything concrete. Most people in her line of business did everything with the intention of looking out for only one person—themselves.

Jesse was just a means to an end.

Sienna continued to stare at him, questions in her gaze.

She was nervous, he realized.

As she should be.

Jesse swallowed hard, knowing she was waiting for his response. He also knew they couldn't stay out here too long without raising suspicions.

He had to make a decision—a decision he could live with.

He released a long breath before saying, "I won't tell Ian about everything that happened leading to this point. But at the first sign you're deceiving me, you better believe everything is coming out. I won't hesitate to take you down."

The breath seemed to leave Sienna's lungs as she nodded up at him. "I'm telling you the truth, Jesse. I promise. The major . . . he was more useful alive than he is dead. Don't you see? This only confirms our theory."

He stiffened. "What theory is that?"

"That a suspicious number of the people surrounding Benjamin Soldier in his final days are now dead."

The next couple of hours felt like a blur.

Sienna talked to the FBI agents and police, and, by all appearances, she kept up her cover well.

But her thoughts still raced through everything that had happened.

Did someone know she and Jesse had come here? Had they followed them and killed the major because of them? Or was the major next on the list anyway?

Sienna still had a lot of questions to be answered. But she and Jesse wouldn't be able to find out any of those answers while they were here.

She slipped into the bathroom and texted Monroe to let him know what was going on. She promised to keep him abreast of any new developments.

But, right now, she didn't know how this situation was going to play out.

She needed to keep her thoughts focused, yet they continually drifted back to the betrayal that Jesse felt. It was stupid that Sienna was letting it affect her this much.

But she was.

She hated the accusation she'd heard in his voice.

But at least Jesse had promised to keep playing along for now. That would buy them some time to get this worked out.

Finally, the medical examiner took the major's body away. An autopsy would confirm his cause of death, but the initial signs seemed to show he'd suffered a heart attack.

Sienna didn't believe Major Benning had died naturally. The timing was too much of a coincidence.

After law enforcement left, Jesse and Sienna turned to Blaine and April as they all stood in the living room. An air of grief hung in the room—grief that would linger for weeks, probably even months.

"I'm so sorry about this, man." Jesse stepped toward Blaine and softened his voice. "I can't imagine what you're going through right now."

Blaine pressed his fingers at the corners of his eyes before shaking his head. "It's going to take a while for me to wrap my mind around this."

"What can we do for you?" Sienna said. "We can get out of here and give you space. Or we can stick around and help you attend to some details. Whatever you need."

Blaine and April glanced at each other.

Finally, Blaine spoke. "Thank you for that offer. But I think right now the two of us just need to be alone."

"We understand," Jesse said. "But I can give you our number and, if you need anything, we'll be here."

"We appreciate that." Blaine extended his hand to shake Jesse's.

"We're going to go grab our things, and we'll be out of your hair," Jesse said. "But I mean it. You need anything, you let us know."

Sienna's lungs loosened as they stepped outside and headed toward the guesthouse.

Jesse didn't say much as they collected their things.

As he started toward the door, Sienna grabbed his arm to stop him. She had something she needed to say, and she didn't want to wait any longer.

"Everything okay?" Jesse asked.

She realized she'd been standing there staring at him instead of speaking. She mentally took stock of the situation.

"I don't know," she finally answered. "I got a message from an old friend. She told me the FBI has launched an internal investigation into you, Jesse."

"What?" A wrinkle formed between his eyes.

"They're taking this allegation that you could be working for the cartel seriously."

"Ian didn't seem to act differently."

She shrugged. "Maybe he hasn't heard yet. But he will. I'm sorry."

Jesse's eyes still weren't especially friendly. He

still thought she could have something to do with the major's death, didn't he?

"I guess I'll have to deal with that later. Now, are you ready to go?"

Feeling as if a weight pressed on her chest, Sienna nodded. "Yes."

"I don't suppose we're going back to the ranch right now, are we?"

"There are still a couple of people we need to speak with."

"Then let's do it." Jesse's jaw hardened as his steely gaze met hers. "If someone did this to the major, I want to know who."

CHAPTER
THIRTY

JESSE AND SIENNA stopped to buy Jesse a new phone. He already felt more in control having one in his possession.

Then he and Sienna grabbed a burger and fries, sitting in the parking lot as they ate and researched Ted Colins.

Ted was an engineer living in Tempe, and nothing Jesse and Sienna read about the man online indicated he might be in some way affiliated with Major Benning or anything that happened overseas.

But the major had gotten that text from the man last night.

What had that been about?

Or maybe the message was unrelated to all of this. *If you know what's smart, you'll do what I say.*

Was someone manipulating the major? Trying to keep him quiet?

"I say we go pay him a visit." Sienna pointed to the man's photo with her fry. "We're already here in this area. What can it hurt?"

It could hurt everything, Jesse mused. But he didn't say that out loud.

He was now intertwined with all this—whether he wanted to be or not. The FBI was investigating him, and someone may have set him up.

It would be prudent to find out as many answers as he could.

Thirty minutes later, Sienna and Jesse pulled onto Ted Colins' street just in time to see him backing out of his driveway and heading in the opposite direction.

They followed him, and a few minutes later he turned into a golf course.

Sienna and Jesse glanced at each other before shrugging, silently agreeing that they could talk to him here just as easily as they could talk to him at his house.

"It's now or never." Jesse put the Jeep into Park.

"I couldn't agree more."

They hurried toward Ted just as he took his golf bag from the trunk of his Tesla.

"Excuse me!" Jesse shouted.

Ted paused and turned, staring at them skeptically.

The man was probably in his eighties with uncountable age spots on his face. He wore plaid shorts and a pale-yellow golf shirt that was tucked in tightly, amplifying his ample belly.

"Do I know you?" Ted stared at them as if preparing himself to fight or to run.

"No, I don't think you do," Sienna said. "But we were hoping to catch up with you."

"And why would you want to catch up with me?" He glanced at his watch as if annoyed. "I have a game to get to. My teammates don't take well to tardiness."

"It's just that we had something to tell you." Sienna tried to carefully choose her words even as she scrambled to come up with a viable explanation. "We know that you were friends with Major Roger Benning, and we're sorry to tell you that he died last night."

Ted blinked several times before setting his golf bag onto the ground of the parking lot.

"What?" His voice came out as an airy gasp.

Jesse offered a solemn nod. "We knew that you

were a close friend of his, and we're trying to let people know."

Ted seemed to process that a moment before his eyes narrowed. "I appreciate that. But . . . this was so urgent that you tracked me down at a golf course?"

"We were going to stop by your house, but we pulled up just as you were leaving," Jesse explained. "That's why we followed you here."

The skeptical look remained in Ted's eyes. "Well, I'm really sorry to hear about the major. But, unfortunately, I haven't talked to him in years."

Sienna sucked in a breath.

That wasn't right.

This man was lying. But why?

In her experience, people usually lied when they were hiding something. And, in this case, the stakes were high.

What exactly didn't Ted want them to know?

CHAPTER
THIRTY-ONE

"WE KNOW you texted the major last night." Jesse decided to get right to the point.

Ted's eyes narrowed, and he took a step back. "I don't know what you're talking about."

"I saw the text with my own eyes," Sienna said. "In fact, your words didn't sound very nice, and I was a little concerned."

"It wasn't like that." He shook his head almost frantically.

"I think we forgot to mention the fact that the major was murdered," Jesse added. "I'm sure the FBI will be reaching out soon to ask you some questions —most likely, right after they check the major's texts."

Ted wiped his brow with a handkerchief from his pocket. "It's like I said, it wasn't like that."

Sienna moved closer, clearly trying to corner the man in his already frazzled state. "How did the two of you even know each other?"

Ted glanced around as if nervous other people might be watching—or that the FBI might be arriving at any time. "We worked together in the army, and I left to work for the Pentagon. When we both ended up in this area, we would touch base on occasion. But I'm telling the truth when I say we hadn't talked to each other in at least five years—not until recently, at least."

Jesse bristled as he realized this man was trying to twist the truth to make himself look innocent. "What happened to change that?"

Ted let out another sigh before glancing around.

The afternoon sun beat down hard on them out here in the unobstructed area. But they weren't going to let that dissuade them right now. In fact, it should only add more pressure on Ted—which was exactly what the man needed.

"Benning approached me about a month ago." Ted wiped his brow again. "I thought he just wanted to get together to catch up, for old time's sake. But it turns out he wanted to write a book."

"A book about what?" Sienna asked, not bothering to hide the surprise in her voice.

Ted shrugged. "Some big exposé on Benjamin

Soldier. I think he thought he was going to make a lot of money from it."

Sienna crossed her arms, her eyes narrowed. "It's been fifteen years. Why do that now?"

"I have no idea." Ted's voice climbed with apprehension. "I didn't even serve with Benjamin, though I did talk to him on occasion. I told Benning I didn't want anything to do with the book."

"That's not how that text sounded," Sienna said. "It sounded like there was more to it."

Ted let out another sigh. "It's complicated."

Sienna squeezed in closer, the look in her eyes unapologetically intimidating. "We have time."

Sienna wasn't leaving here until she had answers. Ted Colins just might be the person to give them the information they needed. He was clearly hiding something.

She waited, letting an uncomfortable silence stretch. Most people didn't like the quiet, and it broke them. She hoped that would be the case with Ted also.

Finally, he let out a sigh and blurted, "The truth is, while I worked for the Pentagon, I had an affair. There? Are you happy now?"

"An affair?" Sienna tried not to show her surprise. But she hadn't been expecting that kind of confession. "I'm still not sure what that has to do with any of this."

Ted's lip twitched down in a partial frown. "Part of what Benning wanted to write about in the book was the affair."

Jesse shook his head as if he was just as perplexed as Sienna. "How was your affair in any way related to Benjamin Soldier and what happened to him?"

"It happens to be that the woman I had the affair with . . ." He let out a sigh before finishing. "She was Benjamin's wife. Benning told me he was going to include that information in the book, that it was an important part of the story."

"His wife?" Sienna didn't bother to hide her distain. "Isn't there a big age difference between the two of you?"

"Forty years or so. But we connected, and . . . it just happened. But I never intended on falling for the woman. I was also married to someone else at the time."

"I take it nobody else knew about this affair?" Jesse asked. "Other than the major."

"That's right. All these years, it was under wraps. Now he comes along and wants to turn all that upside down. Why would he want to do that? Why couldn't he just leave me out of it?"

"Were you anxious about him doing this?" Jesse asked. "Maybe even so anxious that you . . . killed him?"

Ted suddenly went completely rigid. "No. I'm not a killer. I simply told Benning that if he shared my secrets, I would share his."

"What kind of secrets did the major have?" Jesse's heart pounded into his chest as he waited for the man's answer.

"He'd made some bad investments . . . and he was on the verge of losing everything because of it."

CHAPTER
THIRTY-TWO

JESSE AND SIENNA were silent for the first several minutes after they left their talk with Ted.

"That wasn't what I expected," Sienna finally said when they were back in the Jeep with the AC cranked.

"Me neither."

"Do you think this has something to do with the other murders? Do you think that the major discovered secrets about other people that he threatened to share?"

Jesse shook his head. "I really don't know. But something happened with that squadron all those years ago, something big enough that more than one person has been killed. Whoever is responsible has gotten away with this for too long now, and they need to be discovered and stopped before anyone else dies."

"I agree."

"What's your personal stake in this?" He glanced at her, studying her with his gaze. "Why is it so important to you?"

Sienna shrugged. "I think justice needs to be served, and the bad guys shouldn't get away with evil deeds. Is that so strange?"

"It's not strange. But what I do find odd is the randomness of it all. Did someone hire you guys to figure this out?"

She shook her head, a flash of hesitation marring her gaze. "No, it's just something that Charlie asked us to look into."

"You guys must have a lot of respect for Charlie."

"We do. And you'll see why one day."

Jesse didn't respond.

"Should we head back to the ranch?" he finally asked.

"I feel like there's more we should do here," Sienna said. "I told you someone else from the squadron lives nearby—in Tempe. His name is Stephen Gaston. What do you say about giving him a visit?"

"While we're here, it just makes sense."

"Great, let me give you some directions then."

She looked up the address and rattled it off. They were only about ten minutes away.

Maybe this Stephen guy would provide some more leads.

If he was even alive still.

A few minutes later, Jesse and Sienna pulled up to a house located in a neighborhood with cookie-cutter homes that were modestly sized with small, neat yards along crowded streets.

"This is it?" He stared at the off-white house in front of him. "This is where Stephen Gaston lives?"

"That's what my information from Google indicates."

"Okay then." He opened his door. "Let's see if he might be willing to share any information with us. But I'm not holding my breath."

They approached the door, and Jesse knocked.

When no one answered, he shifted to the side and peered through the window. The car in the driveway indicated that someone should be home.

As he glanced through the window, he saw the back door open. "Someone's trying to get away!"

They darted in opposite directions, racing to find the person who'd been inside.

What if it had been the killer?

They needed to catch this person before he got away.

And Jesse prayed that Stephen was okay in the process.

He hurdled a chain-link fence just in time to see someone on the opposite side of the yard also trying to scale the fence.

Jesse grabbed the man's leg before he could jump to the other side.

The man fell to the ground, his eyes wide and his motions shaky.

"Please . . . don't kill me. I beg you."

Jesse stared at the man another moment.

What in the world was this guy talking about?

CHAPTER
THIRTY-THREE

SIENNA REACHED the two men just in time to hear the man on the ground begging for his life.

As she stared down at the fifty-something man, a knot formed between her eyes.

"Stephen?"

She'd expected an intruder or a killer.

But Stephen Gaston had been the one running? She'd seen this man's photo when she'd been online researching squadron members.

"I don't have anything." Panic raced through his high-pitched tone and colliding words. "I don't know anything. And I won't talk. I promise."

Jesse jerked the man to his feet. "We're not here to hurt you."

Stephen brushed grass off his pants before

glancing back and forth between the two of them, looking nearly beside himself. "Then who are you?"

"We were sent to find some answers." Sienna's hands went to her waist. "Some answers about your old army squadron."

"Who do you work for?"

Sienna nodded at Jesse. "He's FBI."

"But I'm not here on official business," Jesse added, determined to set the record straight before he got himself into more hot water.

"I can't talk out here. It's not safe. Those guys could come any minute."

"If you're trying to hide from someone, why are you staying at your house?" Sienna knew that most people fled when they felt they were in danger.

His cheeks heated. "I don't have anywhere else to go. I'm not exactly rolling in the dough, and I don't want to put anyone I know into danger by staying with them."

Jesse glanced around as if looking for trouble—or even just a nosy neighbor. "How about if we go for a ride and talk?"

He stared as if unsure if he was willing to trust them that quickly.

"Major Benning is dead, Stephen."

"What?" Disbelief stretched through his voice.

"It's true. We believe he was murdered. We only want to stop whoever is behind this."

Stephen stared at them a moment, contemplating his actions—and no doubt his future—before he finally nodded. "Okay."

Some of the air left her lungs. "Do you want to take a bag with you? Just in case?"

"Just in case what?" He sounded startled.

"Just in case you need to stay somewhere else— for your own safety," Jesse told him.

His shoulders seemed to relax some. "Okay. Maybe just a few clothes and toiletries. Other than that, I only need my cell phone and wallet. I live here alone, and I don't have any pets."

"Then let's go." Jesse glanced around. "Especially if it's not safe here."

Several minutes later, they climbed into the Jeep and started down the road. Jesse and Sienna both kept a lookout as they traveled just in case trouble found them as Stephen seemed to indicate it could.

Sienna glanced into the backseat at Stephen, desperate for more answers. "It sounds like you've had some threats against you."

"Threats? I'm lucky I got away with my life." He fanned his face as if hot.

"Who's been trying to kill you?" Jesse glanced at him in the rearview mirror.

A frown captured his entire face, from the subtle wrinkles on his forehead to his thin lips. "That's what I would like to know also."

As they headed down the road, Jesse's mind continued to race as he tried to put more pieces together. "So, someone's been threatening to kill you, and you have no idea who or why?"

"That's right," Stephen said. "I thought it was because of my old job, but now I'm not so sure."

"What do you mean you thought it was because of your job?" Sienna turned toward the man from the front seat.

"I used to work at a used car dealership, and I caught my boss doing some backhanded deals so I confronted him. I thought maybe he wanted revenge or something. I went to talk to him, but he seemed honestly clueless. He said he'd turned his life around and that he'd gone to the police about what he'd done. He avoided any jail time by agreeing to pay some people back and putting in community service hours, apparently."

"Do you have any other guesses about who could be doing this?" Sienna asked.

"No, I wish I did." He let out a long breath. "I was

almost run off the road the other day. Then someone broke into my house about a week ago. I noticed the front door was cracked open, so I went back out to my car, and they ran away. But the kicker happened two nights ago."

"What was that?" Jesse asked.

"I was leaving the grocery store when someone came up behind me with a gun and demanded money," Stephen said. "I knew this guy was going to kill me. Before he could, a whole group of cars pulled in—apparently, they were caravanning together on a trip. All those vehicles spooked this guy, and he ran. But I've been on edge ever since. Now, you guys show up. I only assumed you wanted to kill me."

"It turns out that some other people that you've worked with have been recently killed," Sienna told him.

"What do you mean? Who?" He glanced around as if suddenly remembering he was still in danger.

"Other members of your squadron have died recently," Jesse said. "I'm surprised no one told you."

"I don't really keep up with those guys very much. I had no idea, but God rest their souls." He suddenly straightened. "Wait . . . you think they were murdered? Do you think this all has something to do with my time in the service?"

"We think that's a good possibility," Sienna said.

"That's why we came to find you. Not to hurt you, but we're hoping you might know something that would help us find whoever is responsible."

Jesse pulled into a parking lot outside a shopping area. He'd keep his eyes open for trouble while he was here. But he wanted to concentrate on this conversation right now.

"I don't know who would want to kill the guys in my squadron," Stephen said. "That sounds crazy. I mean, I got out of the military ten years ago. Why resurrect the past now?"

"That's a good question," Jesse said. "Anything that you can tell us might be helpful. Anything at all."

CHAPTER
THIRTY-FOUR

SIENNA LISTENED, anxious to get more answers. Anxious to know if this guy was telling the truth. Anxious to know why someone was trying to kill off these men.

Sitting in the parking lot, they ran through the details with Stephen, details about what had happened to the other men.

Stephen seemed to grow paler with each new death mentioned—as would anyone in his shoes.

"Did anything happen with your squadron that someone might want to keep silent?" Jesse pressed. "Especially in the wake of the major writing this book?"

"The major was writing a book?" Stephen shrugged. "That's the first I've heard about it. What about?"

"Your old squadron and Benjamin Soldier, apparently," Sienna said. "It's got some people all up in arms."

"I'm sorry to hear that." He shrugged again.

"Someone has obviously placed a target on all of your backs," Sienna reminded him. "Could it be someone from a village that you guys may have invaded or something?"

"Our enemies over there . . . they were pretty hateful. I mean, I suppose that's a possibility."

"What can you tell us about who you were fighting?" Jesse asked.

"We thought we found the terrorist cell—the ones responsible for the bombing in Florida," he said. "But we were wrong. By the time we realized that, it was too late. The explosives had already been set. We ended up killing two innocent families—a fact that has haunted me ever since."

"I can only imagine." Sienna shifted. "Did anything happen afterward?"

"We got threats. From the father and brother of one of the families. Said they would get revenge on us. But I never saw them again. I figured it was just their grief talking."

Sienna and Jesse glanced at each other.

Maybe they were finally onto something.

But if there was a hitman out there determined to

kill everyone from the squadron, then Jesse and Sienna needed to stop this man before it was too late.

———

Jesse and Sienna took Stephen to a hotel north of Tempe.

They paid for the man to stay there for a week and left him with plenty of groceries to hold him over. Stephen needed to lie low while they figured out who was behind these attempts on his life.

Sienna had called in a favor, and an old friend would keep guard outside the motel tonight, just in case trouble showed up.

"I don't like this," Sienna muttered as they left Stephen and headed back toward the ranch.

"Neither do I." Jesse's gaze hardened. "In fact, it keeps getting worse and worse."

"Agreed."

Jesse stole a glance at her. "Can you look into these guys he told us about? Look into the families that were mistakenly bombed?"

Sienna nodded. "Of course. Charlie has more resources. But, once we're back at the ranch, we'll see what we can discover."

"In the meantime, I guess we head back for now."

He nodded toward the sun sinking in the sky to their west.

"That's a good idea. Are you okay with driving that far?"

He shrugged. "I've always liked being in the driver's seat."

"Somehow it doesn't surprise me that you said that." Sienna let out a chuckle.

He glanced at her. "You also seem like the type who likes to be in charge."

She raised her eyebrows, not bothering to deny it. "That's because I do."

"I don't know . . . I've thought a few times throughout the past couple of days that the two of us actually make a pretty good team." He raised a shoulder as if surprised.

"I agree. Who would have thought?" Certainly not Sienna.

Jesse glanced at the wedding ring on his finger.

Some of those good vibes he'd been feeling suddenly disappeared.

Working well together on one assignment did not change the fact of the matter here.

He had been coerced into marriage against his will.

And now the major was dead. Though Sienna had

sounded convincing, what if she had something to do with his death?

It didn't matter how charming or beautiful Sienna was . . . the whole thing left him with a bad feeling.

Had she truly just been looking out for her own well-being?

Was she telling the truth when she said someone in the FBI had it in for him?

It was a possibility.

As Jesse looked into his rearview mirror, a car appeared there. No, it didn't *appear* there. It had been there for the past fifteen minutes. Following their every turn and move.

Was someone onto them?

That seemed a good possibility.

He glanced over at Sienna. "Hold on. Because things might get a little wild here in a minute."

CHAPTER
THIRTY-FIVE

SIENNA GLANCED behind her and saw the sedan.

Sure enough, they were being followed.

The question was, was it by the person who'd killed Major Benning? Or by the cartel? Or someone else entirely?

"I wonder if we've been followed all day," Jesse muttered, his jaw hardening as he glanced into the rearview mirror again.

"I think one of us would have noticed. Don't you?" They were both trained and astute. But still . . . if these guys were well trained too, they might just be clever enough to conceal their presence.

"They could have been staking out the house when we went to visit Stephen."

Her heart skipped a beat at that thought. "If that's

the case, then Stephen is still in danger. These people know where he's staying."

"This keeps getting worse and worse." Jesse took a hard left, turning into oncoming traffic.

Sienna nearly collided with him at the sudden movement. Instead, she held onto the bar above her and tried to keep herself in place, even amidst the honks from the cars they'd almost hit.

Sienna glanced behind them as they sped away.

The same blue car appeared a moment later.

She frowned.

The vehicle had tinted windows, which made it nearly impossible to see inside.

Sienna glanced at Jesse. "What's your plan?"

"To get away."

"No joke," she muttered. "But how?"

"I'm not sure yet." He glanced in the rearview mirror again. "Any ideas?"

"We need to get away from this populated area. There are too many innocent civilians around us. I don't want anyone else to get harmed."

"Good idea."

She pointed up ahead. "That sign says if you turn off there's a state park. Maybe we should head that way."

As soon as Sienna said the words, he made another hard left.

Cars honked as they dodged them in the oncoming traffic.

But they made it across the street.

"Talk about defensive driving skills," Sienna muttered, still holding on to the bar above her. "You're good."

Jesse shrugged, keeping his eyes on the road. "I might've taken an extra driving class or two."

As they hurried down the road, Sienna saw another sign for the state park. It was only a mile away.

If they could get there . . . and if it was less crowded than this road . . . then maybe there would be a peaceful resolution to this chase.

Sienna grabbed her gun. As soon as no one else was around to get hurt, she wouldn't hesitate to take a shot.

"You know what you're doing with that?" Jesse glanced at her with wide eyes.

"Did you forget I used to be CIA? Or are you only asking me that because I'm a woman? You wouldn't ask that to one of your male colleagues, now, would you?"

"Point taken. You're capable. I've seen that firsthand."

He turned into the state park. Signs near the entrance indicated it was closed for renovations.

Closed?

It was too late to turn back now.

No one was posted at the guard station, so they breezed by.

When the car appeared behind them again, Sienna rolled down her window.

Now it was time to take some action.

Jesse gripped the wheel as he headed down the road.

Now he not only had to worry about the person following them, but he couldn't make any sudden moves that might throw Sienna out the window.

She appeared to know what she was doing as she leaned out with her gun drawn.

The next instant, a bullet blasted through the air.

The car behind him swerved.

Jesse's lungs tightened as someone appeared from the passenger side of the other vehicle.

Also with a gun.

Please don't let anyone get hurt, he silently prayed.

He continued deeper into the park, grateful for the trees on the hills around them.

Sienna fired again.

The car behind them veered toward the edge of the road.

Then the other gunman fired again.

The Jeep lurched.

The bullet must have hit a tire.

Jesse fought to maintain control of the vehicle as orange barrels appeared in front of him.

As he did, he saw Sienna dangerously close to falling out the window.

He reached over and grabbed her waistband, pulling her back inside just as he saw the "Road Work Ahead" sign.

"Put your seatbelt back on. Now!" His hand went to the clutch.

As he dodged the sign, the road in front of them disappeared.

And then they were falling . . . Jesse for the second time in just over a week.

He prayed Sienna had engaged her seatbelt in time.

CHAPTER
THIRTY-SIX

SIENNA FELT the Jeep lurch forward as she clicked the seatbelt into place.

The ground in front of them disappeared and her stomach dropped as gravity pulled them downward.

Everything happened so fast she could hardly process the turn of events.

All she knew was that she tumbled down . . . down . . . down.

Then they stopped.

Sienna held her breath, unable to function as she tried to fathom what had happened.

Tree limbs seemed to grasp the front windshield like fingers. Rocky terrain peeked out beneath the leaves.

And her entire body angled forward, only kept in

place by her seatbelt. Without it she would cascade into the windshield.

"Are you okay?" Jesse glanced at her.

"I don't know." Her voice trembled. "I think so."

"The trees and some kind of ledge must have stopped us."

Sienna remained frozen as she tried to determine whether or not the vehicle was stable. Was this pause just a brief respite? Would they soon tumble forward? Or had they firmly stopped?

The Jeep rocked slightly.

"Jesse . . ." Panic raced through her.

"We need to get out of here." Jesse's voice sounded firm, leaving no room for questions or doubts.

"I think I'm more comfortable staying where I am."

"This car is going to go down. There's a good chance it might catch fire. We have to get out while we still can."

At the thought of cascading farther down the cliff and being engulfed in flames, she nodded. "Okay, what do we need to do?"

"I'm going to slowly open my door. I'm going to climb out, and then I'm going to reach for you. I'm not going to leave here without you. Do you understand?"

Sienna nodded, even though the thought of being left in this car alone—even if it was for only mere seconds—terrified her. Ever since Munich, heights hadn't been her thing.

The Jeep swayed again, teasing them that it could continue on its downward track at any moment.

"I'm going to open my door now." Jesse's voice sounded firm and steady.

She nodded, trying to find courage deep down inside herself despite the fear she felt.

"We've got this." Jesse's gaze lingered on her another moment before he slowly opened the door.

Sienna continued to hold her breath, waiting for the Jeep to continue to plunge.

But it didn't.

Not yet.

Slowly, moving as little as possible, Jesse slipped onto the ledge where the Jeep rested.

Sienna couldn't tell from where he was standing how wide it was or how much room he had.

But at least there was something there. If she wanted to look on the bright side.

"Okay, take your seatbelt off," Jesse coaxed.

Her hands trembled as she released the latch.

"I'm going to need you to take my hand," he said. "I won't let go."

Just as he said the words, the Jeep lurched again.

Sienna screamed.

The Jeep started to slip downward.

Then Jesse appeared again. "I'm here, wifey. Take my hand."

Not even his use of wifey could snap her from her stupor right now. Instead, she tried to catch her breath.

Moving was the last thing Sienna wanted to do.

She didn't want to set this Jeep in motion and create another avalanche of sorts.

"Sienna . . ."

She looked up, and Jesse's gaze locked with hers. "Take my hand."

Something about the confident look in his eyes pulled her from some of her panic, and she nodded. "Okay."

Slowly, she reached forward. Jesse's strong grip caught her hand. Then he grabbed her wrist with his other hand.

Just as he did, the Jeep lurched one more time.

Sienna closed her eyes, convinced she was about to face a certain death.

Jesse felt the Jeep lurch.

And he feared that he might be too late.

His grip tightened on Sienna's arm as the vehicle began to fall.

He quickly repositioned his feet, determined that momentum wouldn't pull him downward.

The Jeep plummeted into nothingness.

But Sienna still clung to his arm.

"I told you I had you . . . wifey dearest," he said.

Her wide eyes proved that she was not finding the situation humorous.

He pulled her up beside him. Instinctually, he put his arms around her and held her.

She was a trembling mess. As anyone would be in this situation.

He gently ran his hand up and down her back in soothing motions. "It's okay. You're okay."

She nearly went limp in his arms. She didn't cry. Didn't say anything. Just clung to him.

Seeing this vulnerable side of her was fascinating. He liked it.

When Sienna let down her guard, she was almost like a totally different person.

Finally, after a few moments, she pulled back slightly and glanced up at him. "Thank you."

"I'm just doing what any good partner would do." Against his better judgment, he reached up and ran his thumb along her cheek.

His gaze went to her mouth. What would it feel like if he pressed his lips against hers?

He wet his own lips, trying to put the thought out of his head.

But it wasn't working.

The longer he held her, the more he wondered what it would be like.

But he was Jesse. Mr. Slick. The one who was never going to get married because it was too complicated. Because the relationships he'd tried had been more of a hassle than they were worth.

Was that because they'd been with the wrong women?

Finally, Sienna stepped back, and the moment was broken.

It was for the best. He knew that. But he was still disappointed.

"We're going to have to figure out a way to get out of this situation," Sienna said.

He glanced up at the cliff face beside them.

It was steep, but not so steep that they shouldn't be able to navigate their way up.

"Do you think those guys chasing us are gone?" Sienna asked.

"Most likely. They saw us go over the cliff and no doubt thought we were goners. I know I did."

"Could you tell who they were?"

"I couldn't. Could have been the cartel. Could have been the person who killed the major. I'm just not sure."

"We'll figure that out later. For now, let's get back up on the roadway and figure things out from there."

CHAPTER
THIRTY-SEVEN

AS JESSE PULLED Sienna up onto the broken roadway, her heart rate finally slowed.

She was on solid ground.

And safe.

For the moment.

She glanced at Jesse again and felt her breath catch.

When he'd looked at her after the Jeep had tumbled down the cliff, a new emotion had stretched through his gaze.

Something that looked an awful lot like affection.

Or was she imagining things? Seeing what she wanted to see instead of the truth?

When Sienna had started this assignment, absolutely no feelings had been involved. And there was no possibility of feelings being involved.

But now . . . she felt something stirring between them.

Something surprising. Unexpected.

And fascinating.

Sienna realized she was staring at Jesse and cleared her throat before brushing some dirt off her jeans. The last thing she needed was for him to catch her looking lovelorn.

Jesse pulled his cell phone out. But, based on his grimace, they didn't have any service here.

He sighed and slipped the device back into his pocket.

"What do you think?" Sienna asked.

He narrowed his gaze as he glanced around. "We're going to have to keep walking until we find service so we can call for help. There should be a signal at the park office."

"Who will we call?"

He studied her face a moment almost as if trying to read her thoughts. "Do you want to call someone from Vanishing Ranch?"

She shrugged. "I would, but they're all awfully far away. The one contact I have in this area is now guarding Stephen."

"I can call one of my buddies with the FBI."

Sienna twisted her head as doubts crowded her mind. "Are you sure you want to do that?"

"I know someone I can trust."

She wanted to ask Jesse again if he was sure. But she didn't want to insult him. However, in this line of work, it was almost impossible to know exactly who to trust. Jesse especially had to feel that way knowing someone at the Bureau had backstabbed him.

But that was a non-issue at the moment.

First, they had to overcome their next obstacle . . . finding a cell signal.

Did Jesse really want to call someone with the FBI?

He kept asking himself that question as he walked down the road toward the park office.

If he was honest, he'd admit he wasn't sure.

He'd run into Ian today, so it was no secret that Jesse was in this area.

In fact, whoever had betrayed him could have already been aware he was in town.

But *who* had betrayed him? That was the question. Could it be Ian?

He and Sienna kept walking down the road. The trees offered some shade from the overbearing heat.

At least, in this situation, he was with Sienna.

Some women wouldn't be doing well right now, considering what they'd both been through. But

Sienna was a trooper who'd proven she could hang with the toughest of the tough.

Jesse tried to imagine what she might have been like as a CIA operative.

She would have been high-octane and formidable, no doubt. He could picture her now in sunglasses and an overcoat. He imagined her in secret meetings. On clandestine assignments.

He fought a smile as he imagined her holding her own in the face of international bad guys. If anyone could do it, Sienna could.

"What are you thinking?" Sienna's voice pulled him out of his thoughts.

No way would Jesse tell her what he'd just been thinking. For so long, he'd wondered if she was the enemy. These new thoughts . . . he didn't quite know what to do with them.

"Just wondering when I'm going to get a signal." He glanced at his phone again.

As he did, one bar popped up on the corner of his screen.

That was it. His pendulant decision. The moment he needed to figure out if calling a colleague would help him or if it would ultimately get him killed.

He already had the one person in mind.

Dan Grimsby.

The two had worked together on several assignments. Once, Dan had even saved his life, throwing Jesse out of the way of an oncoming bullet.

If there was anyone he could trust, it was Dan.

Jesse decided to take a chance.

Quickly, he dialed his friend's number, and Dan answered a moment later.

He paused and stepped toward the trees, where they'd be less exposed. "Dan, it's Jesse."

"Jesse . . . long time no see. To what do I owe the honor of this call?"

"I have a favor to ask of you . . ." Then Jesse spilled the basics of what had just happened to the major.

CHAPTER
THIRTY-EIGHT

SIENNA HAD misgivings about this situation.

She really hoped Jesse wasn't trusting the wrong guy.

Then again, he had years of undercover experience. Certainly, he knew what he was doing.

But that didn't mean she was comfortable with this.

The two of them waited on the side of the road, behind a cluster of trees—just in case those guys either came back to look for them or sent backup.

Thirty minutes after Jesse made his call, a black SUV pulled up near them. A window rolled down, and a man wearing a suit leaned toward them from the driver's seat.

"Dan . . ." Jesse nodded toward the vehicle. "Let's go."

He and Sienna climbed inside, and Dan took off.

After Jesse introduced them, Sienna quickly studied the man, trying to ascertain for herself if he was trustworthy.

Dan Grimsby was probably in his early forties. His hair was cut short. His cheeks were slightly chubby even though the man looked fit. He seemed to have an even personality, like he wasn't the type to fly off the handle or to be the life of the party either.

The next several minutes would determine if this was a good choice or a grave mistake.

"Thanks for coming," Jesse said as he snapped his seatbelt on.

"No problem." Dan continued down the road. "Do you want to tell me what exactly is going on? You both look like you've seen better days."

"We have, and we will tell you more details. But first I need you to take us somewhere we can rent a car."

"Rent a car?" Dan stole a glance at him.

"I'm going to need to get out of this place soon."

Thankfully, Sienna had kept her wallet and phone in her back pockets. She had a company credit card—as well as some cash—that would allow them to do whatever they needed to get out of this situation.

"You're in trouble?" Dan asked.

Jesse shrugged. "You could say that."

Silence stretched for a moment, and Sienna could see Dan was gathering his thoughts.

"You know there's been some chatter about you within the FBI, right?" Dan stole a glance at Jesse, remorse in his tone. "I didn't want to be the one to tell you that . . . but it seems necessary right now."

Jesse's gaze darkened. "I did hear something about that. But you know I'd never get in on these undercover assignments so deep that you guys can't trust me."

"That's what we heard happened. With the cartel. That you'd gone as far as to kill someone."

Sienna sucked in a breath, even though she already knew Jesse had been set up. Hearing the confirmation had to feel like a slap in the face to Jesse.

Jesse visibly bristled. "I would never do that for the sake of the job. You know that. Who started those rumors about me?"

"I can't say for sure." Dan stared straight ahead.

"Then just spitball it for me." Jesse's voice left no room for argument. "I need to know what's happening, Dan."

Sienna listened, anxious to hear what Dan would say.

He remained hesitant as he drove around a curve in the road.

Sienna's gun was still in its holster. She'd had just enough time to secure it before they'd fallen off the cliff.

She hoped she didn't have to use it.

But Sienna wasn't going to lie to herself.

Dan was acting cagey . . . and she for one wasn't willing to blindly trust anyone.

Jesse hated how hesitant his friend was being.

He could understand why Dan had reservations. But, still, this was Jesse's life on the line and his career at stake. This was no time to hold back.

"Peter," Dan finally said. "Peter Stokes is the one I first heard this from. I can't be sure, but I think he went to the supervisor about you also."

"Peter . . . how would he even know any of this? I've barely worked with the guy." Jesse's thoughts ran through everything he knew about the man— which wasn't much. He had heard that Peter wanted to go undercover but had been denied.

Would Peter have resented Jesse because of that? It seemed like a stretch.

"Why would Peter say that? Out of spite?"

Dan shrugged as they continued down the road.

"Why does anyone turn on someone else? It's usually for their own personal gain."

Jesse's thoughts continued to race.

What if Peter was actually working for the cartel? If he'd sold Jesse out for some type of paycheck? Because wasn't that why anyone would do this—for the money?

And Peter, if Jesse remembered correctly, was facing mounting debt after a car accident took him out of work for almost a year.

His stomach knotted.

As it did, he resisted a wince.

He raised his shirt and saw one of his stitches had torn.

"Oh man . . ." Dan did a double take. "What happened?"

"The accident must have aggravated the area. It'll be okay."

"I'm not talking about the stitch that pulled. I'm talking about why you have stitches in the first place."

Jesse pressed his lips together, hesitating only a second before answering. "The cartel sent people to kill me. They thought I was a cop. That means whoever backstabbed me did it knowing I'd probably die."

Dan narrowed his eyes as he headed down the

road. "I don't like the sound of this. You know I've always thought of you as an upright agent."

Jesse rolled his shoulders back. "I am. I don't like lies. That's why I was going to get out of undercover work."

"It's probably for the best. You can only last a certain number of years before you start to lose yourself. At least, that's what I've heard."

Jesse glanced in the back seat at Sienna. "Can we tell him what else we've discovered? This is your rodeo, not mine. But I really think we should."

Her eyes widened as if that was the last thing she'd expected him to ask.

He hoped she trusted him, though.

Besides, someone else other than the two of them needed to know what was going on . . . before either of them were blamed for any of these deaths.

CHAPTER
THIRTY-NINE

AS THEY CONTINUED DOWN the road, Jesse ran through the details surrounding Major Benning's death as well as Ted Colins' and Stephen Gaston's connection.

"I can look into those deaths and see what I can find out," Dan said when Jesse finished. "I agree they sound suspicious."

Jesse's jaw tightened. "There's more to all this. I'm sure of it."

"I'm not certain anyone else has made these connections yet. It's definitely worth researching. If someone is behind this, they need to be caught."

They arrived in Tempe, and Jesse pulled out his phone to search for a rental car agency.

Sienna popped her head forward. "How about a used car dealership instead?"

"Used car?"

"It will be harder for anyone to track us that way."

"Who's tracking you?" Dan glanced back at her.

"The people who tried to run us off the road back there, for starters." Jesse pulled down his visor as the sun blared in his eyes, further putting him on edge. "Someone clearly knows we're investigating, and they don't like it."

"Maybe you should come into the station and give a statement," Dan suggested.

Jesse shook his head as he remembered what Sienna had told him.

Someone at the office could have betrayed him. Someone like Peter.

Someone who'd known Jesse was lying in a hospital room, but who did nothing to protect or help him.

It would be hard to get over that realization.

But Jesse would find whoever had spread lies about him. They wouldn't get away with it.

"There's a car dealership." Sienna pointed to a small, privately owned lot with colorful flags fluttering at the roadside.

Dan pulled to a stop in front of the sales office before turning toward them. "What else can I do for you guys?"

"I think we've got it from here." Jesse released his seatbelt. "But if we could keep all this between us, I'd appreciate it."

Dan nodded stiffly. "Of course. And call me if anything comes up."

"Will do."

With that, Jesse and Siena climbed from Dan's SUV and went to purchase a vehicle of their own.

An hour and a half later, Sienna and Jesse had bought a 1986 Jeep Wrangler and were heading back toward the ranch.

It would be a long drive, but she didn't think they were being followed this time.

That was good news, at least.

"You really think you can trust that guy?" Sienna asked Jesse as he sat behind the wheel.

She'd been wanting to pose that question ever since Jesse had insisted on calling Dan. She didn't want to doubt him—she *didn't* doubt him. But this situation was tough, and trusting the wrong person could get them both killed.

Jesse continued staring at the road ahead. "If I can't trust him then I don't know who I can trust. He saved my life once, and I've never forgotten that.

However, in this line of work, it's hard to be certain about anyone, isn't it?"

"It is." Sienna heard the strain in her own voice.

She knew firsthand just how difficult trust could be.

Jesse stole a glance at her. "You sound as if you know."

She fought a frown. She had been hoping he wouldn't notice, but, of course, he had.

How much did she share about the incidents that had made her into who she was today—the good, the bad, and the ugly of it all? She usually kept those details bottled up inside.

But something about Jesse made her want to open up.

She licked her lips before admitting, "I was engaged once . . . but he . . . well, my fiancé betrayed me."

Jesse stole a surprised glance at her. "Really?"

"Really. He broke my heart." The words burned as they left her lips. The admission wasn't easy. It made her feel weak.

But her statement was true.

"I'm sorry, Sienna. That's the worst kind of betrayal."

"I agree." She tightened her arms across her chest.

"But it's really much easier to go through life without being attached to anyone, you know?"

And there it was . . . her defense mechanism. The walls she'd built up. The lies she told herself.

"Then you find yourself in situations like this, and you realize you have no choice but to depend on others." He glanced her way. "You can trust me, Sienna."

She let Jesse's words hang in the air for a moment.

She knew it didn't make sense. But, against all the odds, Sienna had established a certain layer of trust with Jesse. How ironic that someone she'd coerced into being here was now the same person she was trusting with her life.

But she couldn't help but think that Jesse was one of the good guys. The past couple days had proven that.

She just hoped Jesse's friend Dan was also trustworthy.

"So, what's next?" Jesse asked almost as if sensing that Sienna needed a change of subject.

"That's a good question." She drew in a deep breath, grateful Jesse had switched topics. "Right now, we know that three men died—four men if you include the major. They were all involved with the same operation over in the Middle East."

"Think we can rule out Ted Colins?"

"I think we can safely say that Ted was *not* involved with any of these deaths, even if he did send that text message to the major. Then there's Stephen, who's pretty much scared for his life right now. He very well could end up the next victim."

"Also true."

She frowned. "What we don't have is a lot of suspects."

"The most obvious would be someone affiliated with the military operation."

"I agree," Sienna said. "We're following up with the rest of the squadron members to see if they have alibis for when the major died."

"Plus, there would be support members," Jesse reminded her. "Even if they were on a secret mission, they'd still need help with travel and logistics. Then we have to ask ourselves: what exactly happened on that operation that would warrant the death of so many people?"

"That's something else that we need to figure out," Sienna said. "I can only assume that something went wrong. Maybe something they agreed to keep quiet about. They could have all been sworn to secrecy for all these years."

"It certainly sounds like that could be the case. Maybe someone threatened to expose everyone. So, our next step is just to look into these other guys' alibis, right?"

"That's right. If the same person is trying to kill Stephen right now, that means the killer is in Arizona."

"So, we go back to the ranch, and we regroup. Then, somehow, we figure out who this bad guy is?"

"That's the plan," Sienna said.

Just as she said those words, Sienna's phone rang. Her eyes widened when she saw the number. "It's Blaine."

They'd all exchanged numbers before they left.

"Should I answer?" Sienna said.

"Go ahead. Put it on speaker if you don't mind."

With a touch of hesitation, she did as he asked.

But a bad feeling churned in her gut as soon as she heard his voice.

CHAPTER
FORTY

JESSE'S STOMACH clenched when he heard Blaine on the phone.

Was there an update on his uncle? Maybe about his cause of death?

"Hey, Blaine." Sienna's voice softened with compassion. "How are you and April holding up?"

"We're doing as well as to be expected, I guess."

"I've got the phone on speaker. Jesse is here with me, and he's listening."

"Good." Something changed in Blaine's voice. It almost seemed to deepen. "I was hoping he would be with you. I've been trying to reach him."

"He . . . lost his phone earlier and had to get a new one. We don't have his new device all set up yet." Sienna cast him a look and shrugged.

"Lost" would be a stretch. But Blaine didn't need

to know that Jesse had thrown his cell phone in the back of a moving vehicle in order to throw cold-blooded killers off his tail.

"Is everything okay?" Jesse gripped the wheel, a sense of unease growing in him.

"We don't know what caused my uncle's death yet," Blaine continued. "We're still waiting on the autopsy report, which could take a while, I guess. That FBI agent called me. Special Agent Ian Murphy."

Jesse's grip on the steering wheel intensified until his knuckles turned white. "Is that right?"

"He said that the FBI is looking for you." Under-lying accusation strained Blaine's voice.

Jesse's lungs tightened. "Looking for me? I just talked to one of my colleagues today. He made no indication of that."

"There was something about the way he said the FBI was looking for you . . . it got my mental gears turning."

Jesse's unease grew. "What are you trying to say, Blaine?"

"You didn't have anything to do with my uncle's death, did you?"

Jesse's heart beat harder when he heard the accusation in his friend's voice. He knew how this might look. But his friend couldn't believe this was true.

"Blaine . . . you know I would never do that."

"I mean, the timing is just uncanny, isn't it?" Blaine's serious tone almost turned biting. "You show up in town. End up spending the night. And now my uncle is dead."

"Why would I want to kill your uncle?"

"I'm not sure. That's what I'm trying to figure out."

Jesse rubbed his jaw, not liking where this was going. He wasn't sure he'd be able to convince his friend of his innocence either. Not with so many emotions at play.

"Blaine . . . I didn't hurt your uncle. You know that."

But Blaine didn't respond.

Seconds ticked by. Finally, Sienna asked, "Listen, Blaine. Did you know anything about a book your uncle was writing?"

"A book? What are you talking about?"

"We just ran into someone who said the major was writing a book. It got me thinking—I wonder if that had something to do with what's happening. With the squadron members dying."

"Wait . . . did you think my uncle was behind that?" An incredulous tone filled Blaine's voice.

Sienna licked her lips. "I didn't say that."

"What kind of book are you talking about? A novel?"

"We heard it was a tell-all about his time in the military," Jesse said.

"I don't know what you're talking about. And I don't like where this is going. It almost sounds like you're accusing my uncle."

"We're not, Blaine—"

But before Sienna could finish, the line went dead.

Regret pounded Jesse. Not regret because he'd done something wrong. But regret over everything that had happened.

Now, more than ever, Jesse needed to figure out who was responsible for these crimes—if for no other reason than to clear his name.

As Jesse climbed from the Jeep and onto the dusty soil of the ranch, he quickly stretched his stiff muscles. They'd gotten back just as the sun sank low in the sky. In an hour, it would completely disappear behind the mountains. But, right now, it cast an orange hue over the land.

His ribs ached, but he'd push through the pain. He had no other choice.

Time wasn't on their side right now.

He and Sienna started toward the mess hall. They'd already talked about it, and they'd decided they needed to debrief with Monroe.

But, before they reached the building, a woman stepped from one of the cabanas in the distance.

Jesse grabbed Sienna's arm and jerked her back as alarm raced through him.

"What is it?" Sienna's eyes widened.

He nodded at the stranger in the distance. "That woman . . . I saw her in the restaurant when we met with Blaine. She was watching us."

He expected to see alarm cross Sienna's features as well, for her to go into defensive mode.

Instead, she shrugged. "Oh, her? I've been wanting you two to meet. That's Charlie."

CHAPTER
FORTY-ONE

JESSE BLINKED, unsure if he'd heard correctly. "What? I thought . . ."

"That Charlie was a man?" Amusement flitted in Sienna's gaze. "It's normal. We like to keep people on their toes."

Charlie stepped toward them, hands on her slim hips and a cool confidence about her. Her hair was long and dark with a touch of blonde on the ends, her eyes big and blue, and her skin tone olive.

"You must be our newest recruit." She pulled down her sunglasses to observe him.

"*Recruit* would be stretching it," Jesse said evenly. "I'm Jesse."

She extended her hand. "Charlene Soldier—but everyone calls me Charlie. Nice to meet you."

Realizations collided in his mind. "Wait . . . Charlie *Soldier*?"

"That's right. Benjamin was my father."

More details began to make sense . . . though Jesse still wanted more of an explanation.

He vaguely remembered Benjamin having a daughter when he'd been killed. She'd probably been sixteen at the time. Since fifteen years had passed, that would put her near thirty now.

She was in charge of this operation?

"I like to refer to everyone here as my angels." Charlie grinned as she swung her hand and highlighted the people around her—including Sienna, Monroe, and Hudson.

Jesse's gaze continued to darken.

Charlie's grin dimmed. "Maybe we should all sit down and talk."

"I'd love that."

He had a lot of questions.

But suddenly it made total sense why they were looking into Benjamin Soldier's death.

———

Maybe Jesse would finally get some of the answers he craved, Sienna mused as she sat in Charlie's office with Jesse.

Monroe was there also, standing behind Charlie like a faithful right-hand man.

But Charlie was clearly the one in charge.

"You own this ranch?" Jesse started.

Charlie nodded, remaining composed and professional. "That's right. I used an endowment I received after Dad's death to buy the land outright. I wanted to create a place where people could come to be born again, so to speak. I wanted to help horses at the same time. Thus, Vanishing Ranch was birthed."

"Born again?" he asked. "As in religiously speaking?"

She shrugged stiffly. "Not necessarily—though we support that also. But I take in women—and men —who need to start new lives. My own mother remarried after my father died. My stepfather was an evil man—a devil in sheep's clothing. Though he didn't physically kill her, I do believe the stress he caused in her life is the reason she had a heart attack and died at such a young age—only forty-four."

"I'm sorry to hear that."

"My mom wasn't a perfect woman—not by any means." Sadness floated through Charlie's eyes. "But she still didn't deserve to be treated the way she was."

Sienna wondered if Charlie knew about the affair her mother had with Ted Colins. Most likely, yes. Or, if she didn't know about Ted specifically, she knew about others.

"It stirred a fire inside me," Charlie continued. "My mom, even with her money, felt trapped. I didn't want any women to feel that way, to feel as if they couldn't escape the danger in their lives. I decided to do something about it. So here I am."

"Sounds admirable. But I'm still unsure what this has to do with me and this mission you sent me on."

"Sienna took a few liberties with that." Charlie threw Sienna a knowing look. "But I needed your connections in order to find out answers about what really happened to my father."

"He was killed in hostile fire."

"That's what I was told. But one of his squad members contacted me a couple of months ago and said he had information on my father's murder— things I needed to know and that he'd kept quiet about for entirely too long."

"What did your source say?" Jesse asked.

She raised her chin. "Unfortunately, he never showed, and his phone was disconnected. I began trying to track down members of the squadron and discovered three had died under mysterious circumstances. That's when I became determined to find out answers."

"You think your father was actually murdered by someone other than insurgents?"

Charlie paused as if contemplating how to answer. "I do believe there's more to the story."

"Did you ever find out who the source was?" Jesse asked.

Charlie shook her head. "Unfortunately, I didn't. For all I know, he could be dead."

He crossed his arms. "Certainly, there have to be other people who can help you besides me."

"Probably. But with your FBI background, your undercover work, and your connections, you seemed like a shoo-in. Plus, when we saw things were going south with the cartel, it seemed the perfect time to bring you in."

Jesse's scowl deepened. "You could have asked."

"I know." She laced her fingers together in front of her. "But you would have said no."

Jesse didn't deny it. Was this woman the type who'd sell him out to the cartel just so he'd be in a position to say yes to her?

He didn't know. But he kept that theory in the back of his mind.

Instead, he asked, "Why not just take it to the media? Let them expose the truth?"

"Because I want more answers first. I need to know what happened before I raise any red flags. I didn't want to give anyone a chance to destroy evidence, or whatever it is they might try to hide."

"I suppose that makes sense. But, so far, we haven't really found out anything."

"I was certain Major Benning was behind this," Charlie admitted. "But apparently, I was incorrect. Now, there are only three other guys left on the squadron to talk to."

"We talked to Stephen Gaston today," Sienna said. "Attempts have been made on his life, and he seemed genuinely frightened."

"Did he have any insight to share?"

"He only reinforced what we knew about the bombs over there that killed civilians. He suggested that maybe the families of some of those victims could be wanting revenge."

"Maybe." Charlie narrowed her gaze with thought. "Let's keep reducing our suspects. Someone somewhere knows something. And I want answers. My family deserves answers."

CHAPTER
FORTY-TWO

SIENNA KEPT her steps slow as she and Jesse headed back toward the bunkhouse.

The stars looked amazing as they twinkled in the dark sky, unobstructed by any lights from the city.

She'd really grown to love it here. Part of the reason she loved it so much was because being here she was tucked away from everyone and everything.

But when Jesse left here, this place wouldn't feel quite the same. He'd quickly gained a place in her heart—so quickly it had surprised even her.

They paused by the bunkhouse door, and Sienna turned to him. "I just wanted to say thank you."

He cocked an eyebrow. "For what?"

"You saved me today on that cliff. You were determined not to let me fall, and you didn't."

He shrugged. "I guess I'm the one who got you

into that pickle in the first place when I went off the road. But, of course, I wasn't going to let you go down with that Jeep. What kind of man do you think I am?"

Sienna had grown to see exactly what kind of man Jesse was. He was honorable and strong and loyal—three qualities she truly appreciated.

"I feel bad because I know a lot about you and you don't know much about me." The words burned in her throat, and she didn't want to go any further. Yet, after all they'd been through, she felt like she owed Jesse an explanation.

He didn't say anything. Instead, he waited for her to continue.

"I know last night at the pool I was acting weird," she continued. "The truth is . . . I got out of the CIA because of medical reasons. I was following an asset, and he turned on me. He had a knife, and I tried to fight and get away. But I wasn't able to."

Sienna hesitated only a moment before pulling down the collar of her shirt to reveal the long, jagged scar there.

Jesse winced when he saw it. "Ouch."

"The scar isn't exactly a great swimsuit look, you know? Anyway, I'd been dating someone at the time it happened. I was engaged, actually. When I told you my fiancé betrayed me, it wasn't in the sense that he found someone else and left me." Her voice cracked. "I had a difficult time dealing with the emotional side of it all. Instead of supporting me, he betrayed my trust when he told me my insides were just as scarred as my outside and that he was no longer attracted to me. It made me feel like less than a person."

"Sienna . . ." Jesse's voice sounded so soft that Sienna almost shed a tear at the earnestness in his tone. "I think your insides and outside are equally as beautiful. You know I wouldn't have cared if I'd seen that scar, right?"

She held herself together, trying to push down her emotions at his words. If she stopped now, she might not ever finish.

"It took me a long time to recover after the attack. This guy . . . he almost killed me. His knife hit close to my heart, and I had several surgeries. Needless to say, I was in the hospital for quite a while. The CIA decided I was no longer a good fit for them. They didn't fire me, but they made sure I would want to quit. They gave me the most mundane assignments. I wasn't allowed in the field anymore. It was brutal."

"That's tough."

Sienna nodded. "That's when Charlie found me. I'd met her once at a fundraiser, and we became fast friends. She told me what she was doing and asked me to come here to help. I was at a really low point in my life, and I've been working to put it back together ever since then. I know I come across sometimes as a little glib, but that's only because I've learned to put up walls around myself as protection."

As soon as she said the words, she wished she could take them back. Spoken out loud, it made her feel so exposed. So vulnerable.

"I can only imagine what you must think of me . . ." Sienna added.

Jesse stared down at her, the moonlight glimmering on his hair. He reached for her, and his thumb skimmed the scar along her collarbone. "I think you're perfect."

His words and his touch made her breath catch. Made her heart beat harder, faster. Made her blood feel as if it had been electrified.

It had been a long time since a man had this effect on her. In fact, maybe this was the first time. Because even when Sienna had been engaged . . . she didn't remember the fireworks she felt right now.

She raised her head and saw Jesse leaning close. Her eyes went to his lips, and she wondered what they would feel like pressed against hers. Wondered what his arms would feel like around her waist.

He leaned closer, and Sienna closed her eyes.

Before their lips touched, a chirping sound cut

through the moment.

Sienna stepped back and released a shaky breath.

That was her phone.

She glanced at it and squinted. Then she looked back at Jesse.

"It's Stephen," she murmured, trying to ignore her disappointment. "I better get this."

Jesse felt his throat swell.

He'd almost kissed Sienna.

And he didn't regret it. In fact, the only thing he regretted was the fact that he hadn't been able to.

But when he saw the concern on Sienna's face as she talked on the phone, his thoughts shifted.

She put the phone on speaker, and Stephen's voice came through.

"They found me," he whispered.

Jesse sucked in a breath. "Stephen, where are you right now?"

"I saw some men searching rooms at the hotel. I knew they were looking for me, so I jumped out the back window and ran through some stores behind the building until I reached a neighborhood. I'm hiding between two cars parked on the street right now."

"What about the guard I stationed outside?" Sienna asked.

"I don't know what happened to him . . . I think he's gone."

Her pulse quickened. "Tell us where you are, and we'll come get you. But we're at least three hours away right now."

"I don't think I can wait that long." His words rushed out, colliding into one another.

"We need you to get to somewhere safe," Jesse said. "Is there a store nearby? A large one where you can easily get lost."

"I think there's a Walmart about a mile from here."

"Can you make it there?" Jesse asked. "If so, Sienna and I can pick you up there."

"I'll see what I can do."

"You can do this." Sienna's voice lilted with hope and encouragement. "I know you can. Just keep moving. Get to that Walmart. We'll be there in a few hours."

"Okay," he said. "I'll do my best."

As Sienna put her phone away, she turned to Jesse. "I don't think we're going to be getting much sleep tonight."

"Not at all. We need to go." He nodded toward the Jeep. "There's no time to waste."

CHAPTER
FORTY-THREE

AS THEY HEADED BACK to Tempe, Sienna wished she could grab an hour of shut-eye. But sleeping wasn't in her nature—not in circumstances like this.

Sure, it was late. She'd probably regret not resting later.

But right now, her mind continued to race, and urgency kept her alert.

"Maybe we shouldn't have left Stephen," she murmured. "I keep trying to call Larry, the guy I left outside. He's not answering."

"I don't know how these people followed us and found Stephen." Jesse's jaw tightened as he stared at the road ahead. "We were careful. I just assumed the people following us today were the cartel. But maybe they had something to do with Benjamin Soldier's death instead."

Sienna released a long, pent-up breath. "We have to narrow down our suspects. This can't go on. We can't let whoever's behind this continue to hurt people."

"I agree. The best thing we can do is to keep looking into the other men on that squadron. Or the family of the people whose house was mistakenly bombed. They seem like the most likely suspects here."

"I agree. But first, let's make sure that Stephen is safe."

The next several miles passed in silence, darkness surrounding them. It reminded Sienna of a mission she'd done in Dubai. She'd traveled all night with sensitive information that she had to get to an ambassador before daybreak. The highly classified nature of the intel made it so she couldn't tell him over the phone or even in writing.

She'd gone forty-eight hours without sleep, only able to stay awake because of adrenaline and too much coffee. In the end, she'd been successful. She hoped she could say that this time also.

Finally, she and Jesse pulled up to the Walmart where Stephen had said he'd meet.

Sienna tried Stephen's cell phone as soon as they pulled into the lot.

"He's not answering," she muttered, her pulse ratcheting a notch.

"That's not good."

"No, it's not. The only reason I can think of that he wouldn't answer . . . well, it's not good."

Wasting no more time, she and Jesse climbed from the Jeep and hurried inside.

Jesse was on edge. Those people going after Stephen could be here now. Could be watching them.

And it was getting late. There weren't that many people inside the store.

On one hand, that was a good thing because it meant innocent bystanders wouldn't be harmed.

On the other hand, that didn't give Stephen the safety or anonymity of crowds.

Why wasn't the man answering his phone? It made no sense.

Unless Stephen had been taken.

Jesse prayed that wasn't the case.

He and Sienna had split up so they could look for the man. But so far, Jesse hadn't seen him anywhere.

He scanned the aisles until he reached the back of

the store. He even checked the men's restroom in case he'd hidden in there.

But Stephen was nowhere to be seen.

Jesse met back with Sienna, and she shared the same update.

Stephen appeared to be gone—if he'd made it there at all.

"What now?" Sienna stared at him, trepidation in her gaze.

She felt personally responsible for this, didn't she?

Jesse placed his hands on his hips, and he glanced in the distance. "What are the odds management will let us see security camera footage?"

"Not good, but it's worth a shot."

They hurried to the customer service counter and asked for the manager. A forty-something man appeared from a back office with a weary look in his eyes. "Can I help you?"

"Our friend called saying he was in danger, and he was supposed to meet us here." Sienna's voice trembled as if she were frightened. "Now we're here to pick him up, and he's nowhere to be found."

"Did you try calling him?"

"Of course, we did. He's not answering. Has anyone reported anything unusual happening in the store?"

He shook his head. "No, it's been quiet tonight."

"Can we see your security footage then? I'm afraid something may have happened to him."

The manager remained unaffected and emotionless. "How about if you call the police instead?"

"We would." Sienna nibbled on her bottom lip, as if trying to show her vulnerability in hopes the manager might be more compelled to help. "But you know how the cops are with missing persons, especially when they're adults. They've got to be gone at least twenty-four hours before the police will even do anything. But we know that every second counts."

"And how do you know that exactly?" The manager's wary gaze stared at them, and he looked like he'd rather do anything than have this conversation.

Okay, this guy wasn't going to make this easy, Jesse mused.

It was time for Plan B.

Sienna glanced at Jesse, clearly trying to tell him something. A moment later, she slipped something into his hands beneath the desk.

He glanced down and saw his wallet—and his badge.

She'd had this with her the whole time?

It didn't matter. Not right now.

Jesse felt the familiar weight of his credentials and

his tone automatically held more authority. "I'm with the FBI. Although I'm not here on official business, I would appreciate your cooperation."

The manager stared at him another moment before nodding. "Fine. You can come look at the security footage. But I'm not going to have time to hold your hand and walk you through this."

A surge of victory rushed through Jesse, and he prayed this would offer some answers.

CHAPTER FORTY-FOUR

SIENNA PAUSED THE SECURITY VIDEO.
"There's Stephen."

The footage from an hour earlier showed a man escorting Stephen away from Walmart. The man forced Stephen into a black truck before taking off.

At least, they knew what had happened.

The bad news was that someone had taken him.

Sienna and Jesse struggled to try to make out the numbers and letters on the license plate, but they had no luck. The video was too grainy.

She turned to Jesse, fighting discouragement. "What should we do now?"

He rubbed his jaw as he leaned back in his chair, still staring at the video monitor in front of him. "Maybe I should consult with one of my contacts with the FBI and send this video to them."

More anxiety rose inside her, nearly choking her. "I'm not sure that's a good idea—not until you know who's turned on you. You can only assume it's Peter, but you don't know for sure."

His jaw hardened. "Maybe I can call my colleagues and ask them for help all while knowing that someone is stabbing me in the back. Maybe this would even flush out whoever betrayed me. As long as we're careful . . ."

A frown tugged on her lip. "I don't know . . . maybe we should sleep on it and figure it out in the morning."

"If we sleep on it, there's a good chance that Stephen will be dead by morning." Jesse's words hung in the air.

She knew what he'd said was true, but . . . "We could drive around this city all night without finding that black truck. We'll just be wasting our time and energy. There has to be a better way."

"Maybe we should try to call Stephen one more time."

Sienna nodded and put the phone to her ear, not expecting anyone to answer.

But to her surprise, the phone went silent on the third ring.

"Hello?" Sienna gripped the phone tight. "Stephen?"

"We have your friend," a deep voice said. "Unless you back off, he's going to die. Understand?"

The line went dead before Sienna could say anything.

Jesse had overheard, and he and Sienna just stared at the phone, letting that sink in.

Clearly, they weren't going to be able to let this go.

But the men who had taken Stephen didn't have to know that.

"We have to figure out our next step." Sienna turned to Jesse. "We can't let them hurt Stephen."

"I'll call someone at the FBI. Maybe they can track Stephen's phone."

"It's risky . . ."

"It's a risk I think we have to take. I can call Dan. He'll help."

"Why not Ian?"

"I don't know him well enough. He seems trustworthy, but Dan has had my back on more than one occasion."

She hesitated a moment before nodding. "Okay then. Let's do it."

Jesse made the call, and Dan promised to look

into it. He called back five minutes later with an address.

"Let's go!" Jesse started back to the Jeep.

Sienna typed the address into her phone and rattled off directions.

But when they arrived, nothing was around— only an open stretch of space waiting for a new neighborhood build. After searching in the area a few minutes, they located the phone in a patch of grass.

It had clearly been discarded. As a way to throw them off? Quite possibly.

Sienna frowned as she turned to Jesse. "What now?"

He rubbed his jaw. "It's too long of a drive to go back to the ranch for the night. We should get a hotel room and get some rest. Then in the morning, we'll start fresh. It's all we can do."

Twenty minutes later, they found a pay by cash hotel on the edge of town. It wasn't the best accommodations, but it would work. They'd share a room tonight—a room with two separate beds. They'd already grabbed some sandwiches, chips, and drinks from a convenience store down the road and had downed part of the food on the drive here.

As soon as they stepped inside, Jesse collapsed back in the bed. He wished he could say he would get some rest tonight. But he knew that would be nearly impossible.

Sienna gently lowered herself onto the bed beside his, looking equally as exhausted. But there was more to her gaze than that. She almost looked . . . apologetic.

Exactly what was going through her mind right now?

He waited for her to speak, sensing she might need some time to sort through her thoughts.

"Jesse . . . I'm sorry about the whole marriage thing." She stared at him pensively.

"That legally binding contract is null and void, right? You said it was just paperwork and your friend can make it disappear."

She nodded, that same heavy look remaining in her gaze. "That's right. Marriage really did seem like the only way to get you out of the hospital safely. But I shouldn't have made light of everything."

"And it was a great way to keep me around so I could help."

She shrugged. "Maybe that too. But still . . . can't you just let a girl say she's sorry? Besides, I kind of like having you around."

"Oh, yeah?" Jesse grinned, fighting the urge to reach over and feel her skin against his.

But that would be a very bad idea in this situation.

Instead, he said, "In that case, you're forgiven."

Her shoulders seemed to slump with relief. "Thank you."

He would like to continue this conversation, but he really needed to get some rest before he sat here and stared at Sienna for too long. "We should probably turn in for the night."

She nodded. "We can talk more in the morning."

He pulled the covers back so he could climb under.

But all he could think about was the sincere look on Sienna's face.

She really was sorry she'd married him, wasn't she?

Oddly enough. He wasn't sure how he felt about that.

CHAPTER
FORTY-FIVE

JUST AS HAD HAPPENED the night before, Sienna tossed and turned for most of the night, unable to fall asleep. Which was too bad because she knew she needed to be sharp today.

Finally, at 5:30, she slipped out of bed and hopped into the shower. Maybe some warm water would help get her moving. After she dressed, she stepped out of the steamy bathroom and paused in her tracks when she saw Jesse sitting up in bed with sleepy eyes and tousled hair.

Her throat went dry at the sight of him. "Good morning."

"Morning." He ran a hand through his hair. "How'd you sleep?"

"Not good. You?"

He let out a breath. "I didn't get much sleep

either, probably because we have a big day ahead of us."

Yes, they did. Today, they had to find Stephen and get him away from those thugs. "You better get in that shower and get ready yourself."

"Yes, ma'am." Jesse gave her a lazy grin as he walked past her into the bathroom.

A lazy grin that had Sienna's pulse racing.

But she didn't have time to think about her reaction. Instead, she continued about her routine, trying to come up with a plan for the day. She pulled out her computer and began researching the other guys from the squadron, trying to find any information on them.

As much as she wanted to find Stephen first thing, they had to have some place to start.

When Jesse emerged from the bathroom fifteen minutes later, she had an update to share with him.

"Willie Tulsa has been out of town for the past three days," she announced as she sat cross-legged on the bed.

"I take it he was in the squadron with Benjamin?"

"That's right. He lives in Michigan now. But I checked his social media, and he's been offline. I did some more research and discovered that he works for a concrete company. With the time difference, I was able to call the company a few minutes ago and ask for him. The receptionist said he'll be out of the office until the beginning of next week."

Jesse lowered himself onto the edge of his bed, still towel-drying his hair in a way that made Sienna's thoughts blitz out until she had to look away.

"I'm going to call one of my colleagues," he announced.

Sienna's eyebrows shot up, and all her other thoughts disappeared. "Are you sure that's a good idea?"

"No, I'm not." He shook his head. "But I can't stop thinking about it. I don't want to run from the accusations against me. I need to talk to someone about what's been going on within the FBI and find out some answers."

"You want to do that now?"

"We need to have the FBI on our side right now. I just need to explain myself and sort this all out. If we have their resources behind us, we'll be much more likely to track down Stephen before something happens to him."

"But Dan already knows . . ."

"We need more than Dan and Ian. I need to clear my name."

She stared at him a moment before nodding. "If that's what you think you need to do, then okay."

But she worried that Jesse was wrong.

Then again, there were very few people she would trust in this situation . . . and maybe that was to her detriment.

Jesse knew Sienna didn't agree with his choice, but he appreciated that she respected him enough to go along with it.

He was able to reach Matthew Patterson, who agreed to meet with him in three hours. Jesse had chosen a location near Prescott, knowing a more wooded area would offer more privacy than the open expanse of the desert. It would be about an almost two-hour drive, but the location would be worth it.

Jesse went to the Jeep by himself. He knew he and Sienna were probably being watched right now, and, because of that, they had to plan their moves carefully.

While he drove down the street, Sienna traveled by foot. As he rounded the corner and pulled into a fast-food drive-through, she jumped into the back-seat and remained low, out of sight.

If they timed things as they planned, no one would know Sienna was with him.

Jesse ordered two sausage biscuits and a couple of

orange juices before driving away and glancing at his watch.

They should arrive right on time to meet Matthew.

Jesse's gut tightened as he thought through possible scenarios. He really hoped he didn't regret this.

In Prescott, he pulled off onto a side road and stopped. He quickly turned to Sienna, knowing they couldn't talk long and give away their cover.

"Are you going to be okay?" he asked.

She nodded. "As soon as it's clear, I'll head out to keep an eye on things for you."

Something about the trustworthiness in her gaze did something funny to his stomach.

There were very few people in life he trusted.

But for some reason, Sienna was quickly becoming one of them.

With one more glance at her, he stepped out and closed the door.

Now it was time to meet Matthew.

He prayed his colleague would listen. That he would be of help.

But in truth, Jesse had no idea how this meeting would play out.

CHAPTER
FORTY-SIX

AFTER FIVE MINUTES HAD PASSED, Sienna poked her head up and glanced around.

No other cars were in the parking lot.

Moving quickly, she climbed out and darted into the woods.

She ducked behind a tree just as another car pulled into the lot.

Was that Matthew?

She'd looked the man up this morning. Knew what he looked like.

But the man who climbed from the sedan wasn't Matthew.

It was someone she'd never seen before.

Based on his hiking boots and cargo shorts, he wasn't somebody with the FBI.

After grabbing a walking stick and backpack out of his back seat, the man started down a trail.

When he was gone, Sienna hurried deeper into the woods.

She knew approximately where Jesse was meeting his former boss.

Now she needed to get to a good position to post herself and watch, just in case Jesse needed a hand.

She was keenly aware of the gun holstered at her ankle.

She wouldn't hesitate to use it if she needed to.

But she really hoped it didn't come down to that.

She watched as Jesse sat on a bench.

Though he was very much alert, his eyes were downcast.

This whole situation was weighing on him, wasn't it?

She wished she could ease some of his burden. But she couldn't. This was his battle. She would be there to support him, to back him up, but these were his decisions.

She knew what it felt like to be betrayed. To have an organization that you have dedicated your life to turn their backs on you.

It wasn't a good feeling.

The sense of betrayal cut deep.

She also understood his need to find the truth.

To find justice.

Just as a figure appeared farther down the trail, she squinted.

Was this it? Was that Matthew?

They were about to find out.

Jesse glanced at his watch again. Matthew was ten minutes late.

That wasn't like him.

He wondered if his colleague had changed his mind.

He wasn't going to make a call. Not yet.

He'd wait five more minutes before making any decisions.

As he waited, Jesse glanced through the woods and tried to spot Sienna.

But he didn't.

Hopefully that was because she was great at remaining unseen, not any other reason. He prayed nothing had happened to her.

Before he could dwell on those thoughts anymore, a figure appeared down the trail.

He stiffened.

Then his shoulders went rigid.

It wasn't Matthew who walked his way.

It was . . . Dan Grimsby.

Jesse rose to his feet, his muscles bristling. "Dan? What are you doing here?"

His colleague paused in front of him. "Matthew couldn't come—he got called out on a special assignment—so he sent me."

Instantly, Jesse's suspicions rose. "Is that right?"

"He said you sounded like this was urgent, and he didn't want to leave you hanging."

Jesse felt himself bristle. "I told Matthew not to tell anybody about our meeting. He could've called me."

Dan shrugged. "He said he didn't want to make you wait. Said you needed help, that it was life or death."

Jesse didn't like the feel of this situation. He found it hard to believe that Matthew would have told Dan these things.

But if Matthew hadn't told him, then how did Dan know about this meeting?

Jesse wasn't sure.

But something smelled rotten.

Had Dan done something to Matthew?

He didn't know what was going on, but he needed to be on guard—especially with danger closing in.

CHAPTER
FORTY-SEVEN

SIENNA COULDN'T BELIEVE her eyes.

Why had Dan come?

She crept closer in time to hear Dan say that Matthew couldn't be here.

But she didn't buy the idea that Matthew had sent Dan instead.

Jesse was being set up right now, wasn't he?

Her heart pounded harder.

Sienna waited.

It wasn't time for her to act. Not yet.

"Dan . . . we both know Matthew didn't send you." An edge formed in Jesse's voice.

Dan's gaze darkened. "Why else would I be here?"

"Why don't you tell me that? Are you the one who made the accusations against me? Not Peter?"

The next instant, Dan drew his gun and aimed it at Jesse. "You just couldn't let this go, could you? I didn't want to have to do this."

Jesse rose up to full height, his voice hardening. "No, you wanted the cartel to finish me off instead. But why? Why are you setting me up?"

"They gave me a deal I couldn't refuse."

"You sold out to the cartel? For money?" Jesse shook his head as disbelief caught his voice. "I thought more highly of you."

"I'm working my butt off for the FBI. I put my life on the line every day. And for what? I'll never have a nice house or a nice car or be able to take the kind of vacations I deserve. Meanwhile, criminals are living the life I want."

"You knew when you signed up for the FBI what you were getting into. That's no excuse."

"I don't need a lecture from you!" Dan's voice rose. "I'm just trying to finish what the cartel messed up before everything is ruined. I know you came here without backup. I followed you. Now you're going to walk. Deeper into this forest."

Good, Sienna mused. Let him think he had the upper hand.

He'd soon find out otherwise.

She slipped the gun from her holster and cocked it.

"I'm not going to walk deeper into the forest." Jesse remained planted near the bench. "I'm not going anywhere with you."

Sienna knew that was her cue to act.

In one motion, Jesse swung his leg and kicked the gun from Dan's hands.

But as he reached down to grab it, two other guys appeared.

Cartel members.

Dan was definitely in deep.

He'd probably been getting kickbacks from these guys in exchange for his silence. In exchange for him turning a blind eye and pretending like he didn't know what was going on.

As one of the guys grabbed Jesse's arm, Dan snatched up his gun and grinned. "You didn't think it was going to be that easy, did you?"

Jesse froze.

"Move!" Dan yelled.

Just as Dan shoved Jesse toward the woods, a bullet sliced the air.

The men around him ducked.

Sienna emerged.

She didn't hesitate to pull the trigger again.

A bullet hit Dan square in the shoulder, and he fell to the ground.

The other guys scrambled. Shot back.

Sienna ducked behind a tree and out of sight.

Jesse stepped on Dan's wrist, tore the gun from his grasp and pointed it at him.

But now they were all in a standoff.

"This isn't going to be the last man standing now, is it?" Jesse asked.

As the words left his mouth, Sienna darted from behind a tree. Swung her leg out. Knocked a guy down.

She stepped on the man's arm, pressing her weight into him. As he cried out in pain, she grabbed his gun.

Jesse took the opportunity to throw a punch at the other guy, pushing the barrel of his gun toward the woods.

The weapon discharged, and a bullet lodged in a nearby tree.

Jesse slammed the butt of his gun on his assailant's head, and the man fell to the ground.

Then he turned back to Dan.

The man moaned on the ground and tried to sit up but failed. "You shouldn't have done that. You're going to regret it."

"I'd say that you're the one making bad decisions." Jesse shook his head as he looked down at the man in pity. "You shouldn't have started those rumors about me. Tried to make it look like I was the one who was helping the cartel. It's just dirty. And I thought we were friends."

He winced with pain. "There are some things in life more important than friends. Like money. Money never lets me down."

"Then you live a sad, sad life," Jesse muttered.

He and Sienna paused. Looked at each other. A silent conversation passed between them.

Was this part really over?

CHAPTER
FORTY-EIGHT

JESSE GRABBED his phone and dialed Ian Murphy's number. He didn't know who to trust, but Ian seemed like the next logical person to get involved right now. He hoped he didn't regret it—and he hoped Matthew was okay.

Backup was on the way. Hopefully, his colleagues would get the whole story now, and Jesse would be cleared.

With his gun still raised as he kept an eye on their attackers, Jesse stepped closer to Sienna. "Good work."

She flashed an adrenaline-fueled smile his way. "I know I've said this before, but I really do think we make a pretty good team."

"I'm inclined to agree. But this isn't over yet. Not by a long stretch."

Her grin slipped. "I know. We need to find out what happened to Benjamin Soldier. Figure out why these guys are dying. And we need to find Stephen and Larry."

"I have an idea. But I can't talk to you about it until we're alone." Jesse glanced around.

"Can't wait to hear what you have in mind."

Fifteen minutes later, the FBI flooded the scene, led by Special Agent Ian Murphy.

As the men were arrested, Jesse and Sienna explained to Ian what happened.

"Jesse set me up," Dan yelled as two agents handcuffed him and led him away. "Don't believe anything he says!"

Ian ignored him and addressed Jesse instead. "We've actually been investigating Dan for a while. What we weren't sure about was whether or not you were working with him."

"I wasn't." Jesse raised his chin. "And I wouldn't do that."

"I personally didn't think you would. However, I had to be sure."

"I appreciate the vote of confidence. But I called Matthew. He was supposed to come."

"Dan must have overheard Matthew on the phone. He told him he would meet you instead.

Matthew was suspicious after the conversation, so he told us."

"Thank God for that." Jesse shifted. "And, just to let you know, Stephen Gaston—another squadron member—is missing, as well as a man named Larry who was guarding Stephen."

"We'll look into that." Ian shifted. "I'd also like to talk to you more back at the FBI office. I understand you want to get out of the undercover work."

"I do. But I have something I need to finish first. Can it wait until tomorrow?"

Ian shifted, his eyes narrowing as he studied Jesse. "Does what you're finishing happen to involve Major Benning?"

Jesse nodded, knowing that withholding the truth would only hurt him right now. "It does. I need to find out what happened to him."

"We have our guys working on it," Ian assured him.

"I know. But I'm invested in this. There's a lead I want to check out. It's urgent."

Ian stared at him a minute before nodding. "Fine. Go . . . but keep me updated."

Wasting no more time, Jesse grabbed Sienna's hand, and they hurried toward the Jeep.

"What's going on?" Sienna asked as they took off down the road.

Jesse clearly had something on his mind—an idea —and she was anxious to hear what it was.

"Remember when we stayed in the major's guesthouse?" Jesse started.

Sienna's cheeks heated as she remembered staying there, as she remembered realizing for the first time how attracted she truly was to Jesse. "I do."

Excitement caught in his voice. "When I was lying in bed and couldn't sleep, I noticed that one of the ceiling tiles wasn't lying in the bracket correctly. It drove me crazy as I stared at it all night."

"Okay. . ." She had no idea where Jesse was going with this.

"When April showed us the guesthouse, she said that the major liked to go out there to think about life. What if he was writing his book out there?"

Her eyebrows shot up as she considered that thought. "You think the major has a copy of his manuscript in the ceiling?"

"If he was sharing explosive things like I think he was, then maybe he hid it there. Maybe he didn't want anyone to find it because he knew how revealing it was."

Sienna chewed on that thought another moment.

"But wouldn't the manuscript be on his computer anyway?"

"Maybe. But the major was old school. He could have handwritten the book. Or he could have even erased the files from his computer and only kept a hard copy. Maybe he knew something was going on, that someone had secrets they didn't want spilled."

"You might be onto something. Should we call Blaine?"

Jesse shook his head. "I don't want to tell anyone about this. Not yet—just in case we're wrong."

That was probably a good idea. "So, what's your plan?"

"I'd like to go back to the major's place and sneak into the guesthouse. I want to see if my theory is right."

Sienna nodded. "I'm on board with that. Let's go."

CHAPTER
FORTY-NINE

JESSE FELT trepidation rising in him as they drove back to Major Benning's place.

He wanted to figure out what had happened to his old friend. He wanted to clear his name. To let Blaine know he would have never hurt the major.

But going back was risky. It could make him appear to be even more guilty.

But what other choice did they have right now?

As far as he was concerned, none. They had no other options.

He and Sienna pulled onto the road leading to the major's home, and Jesse slowed.

The driveway was empty—but that didn't mean there wasn't a car in the garage. Since Blaine and April were busy with their startup, that could mean they worked from home.

Jesse pulled to a stop behind a few small trees that would conceal them—at least at first glance.

They'd go the rest of the way on foot.

"You ready for this?" he turned to Sienna, knowing that this was risky—and that it might not prove anything.

She nodded. "I'm ready to find some answers."

They remained on the side of the road as they headed toward the major's place. Once they reached his property, they skirted around the backside of it.

So far, Jesse hadn't seen anyone, and nothing indicated anyone was home—no sounds or lights or movements.

Still, they would need to be careful.

They scaled the iron fence surrounding the property and landed on the other side behind the guesthouse. Remaining low, they rushed toward the door.

It was locked. Jesse tried the code they'd been given when they stayed there, and it worked.

Once inside with the door closed, he glanced around.

His gaze stopped on that crooked ceiling tile.

This could be nothing.

Or it could be everything.

"You can do the honors." Sienna nodded toward the ceiling.

Jesse hesitated only a moment before walking to

the couch and stepping onto the cushions. Balancing himself, he reached up and nudged the white ceiling tile back.

He slid it out of the way before reaching into the space, unsure what his fingers would touch.

Nothing at first.

And then . . . papers.

His heart rate kicked up a notch.

Carefully, he reached farther into the ceiling and grabbed them. As he pulled them in front of him, he realized he held the missing manuscript.

His gaze met Sienna's.

This was it.

The moment of truth.

They'd found it.

Sienna could hardly believe her eyes.

This was Major Benning's book. The words inside could contain the answers they needed to pinpoint who was behind these killings.

Jesse set the manuscript on the small dinette beside them and stared at the title.

Forgotten Secrets.

He picked up the page and began reading aloud. "There are many things I've learned through my years of military service. But the most important one is this: it's hard to know who to trust. I believe that Benjamin Soldier was murdered and that someone in the very government he served put this plan in place. I've spent the last fifteen years of my life trying to figure out what really happened, and now I finally know the truth. It's time for the rest of the world to know also."

Sienna's gaze met Jesse's. "So, he's saying Benjamin Soldier's death was a setup by someone in the government—or by one of his colleagues? That the terrorist cell wasn't responsible?"

"That's what it sounds like to me." His stomach churned at that revelation.

"But why would someone want to kill Benjamin Soldier?"

"We find that answer, and we'll probably find our killer."

Before they could read any more, something clicked behind them.

Sienna swung her head toward the sound and saw someone standing in the doorway.

With a gun.

Pointed at them.

CHAPTER
FIFTY

JESSE FELT the breath leave his lungs as he stared at the figure standing there. "April? What are you doing?"

The woman had transformed from classy and understated to someone full of vengeance.

"I've been looking for that," she muttered as she nodded toward the book. "I didn't think Major Benning hid it out here. I searched everywhere. Where did you find it?"

"It doesn't really matter, does it?" Jesse placed the pages onto the table and turned toward April, knowing how quickly this situation could escalate. "I don't understand why you're here. Why you're holding a gun. Why it's pointed at us."

Her gaze darkened. "I need that manuscript. It

can't be released. If it is, my brother will go to jail for the rest of his life. I can't let that happen."

"Who's your brother?" Confusion marred Sienna's tone.

"Richard Birdwell."

Jesse squinted at the name. "Richard? We looked into him when we researched members of the squadron. He's significantly older than you are. And Blaine never mentioned a connection . . ."

April's nostrils flared. "I didn't know Richard was my brother until five years ago. We had different mothers but a similar childhood experience—full of trauma and neglect. We instantly bonded when we found each other, especially since neither of us had any other family—decent family, at least."

"Does Blaine know about your connection to Richard?" Jesse asked.

She shook her head, an almost crazy, disconnected look in her gaze. "No, I didn't tell him. He didn't need to know."

"Wait . . ." Sienna twisted her head. "Did you marry Blaine just for his connection with the major? You married three months ago. It wasn't long after that some of these mysterious deaths began happening."

April's gaze hardened, and the gun trembled in

her hands. She was a woman on the verge of losing it.

Based on what Jesse had put together, bad things happened when April lost it.

Murderous things.

"That could have been part of it," April snapped. "But you don't understand what's going on here. You can't possibly understand all the implications of this book or what my brother has been through."

"Why don't you explain it to us?" Jesse needed to buy some time until he figured out how to get that gun from April.

Her eyes narrowed even more. "There's no time for that now. I need that book. Then I need to figure out what to do with you two. We don't have much time here."

"Are you going to kill us, just like you killed those other people?" Sienna's voice sounded strangely calm.

Her words echoed in Jesse's head.

Was Sienna right? Was April the killer here?

Jesse's heart beat harder.

He thought he was a good judge of people. But April hadn't even been on his radar.

"I don't know yet!" April snapped. "You two weren't supposed to come back. Things weren't supposed to end up this way."

"How were they supposed to end up?" Jesse asked calmly.

"I just want to protect my brother. People are going to think he killed Benjamin Soldier . . . but he didn't."

Just as she said the words, someone else stepped into the room.

Blaine.

And things suddenly became even more complicated.

"What's going on here?" Blaine's eyes swiveled around the room as confusion buried itself in his gaze.

"I found them in here." April's voice took on a helpless, almost desperate sound. "They're in on this, Blaine. It's their fault the major is dead."

A knot formed on his brow. "Who? Jesse? Sienna?"

"Of course!" April swung her hands in the air in overexaggerated motions. "Who else would I be talking about?"

April was definitely losing it, Jesse mused. But he stayed quiet . . . for now.

"And you happened to bring your gun with

you?" Bewilderment lilted Blaine's voice. "I don't understand . . ."

She scowled. "I thought I heard someone out here, so I came to check it out."

"You should have gotten me." Blaine's lips twitched in a frown. "What if it had been someone dangerous?"

"None of that matters! Can't you see that! These people—your supposed friends—broke into the guesthouse."

Blaine's gaze turned back to Jesse and Sienna as his thoughts seemed to shift. Suspicion lined his eyes and the firm set of his mouth. "She's right. What are you two doing here?"

Jesse raised his hands. "Let me explain. It's not what it looks like."

The gun waivered in April's hands. "There's no time for them to explain, Blaine. They're here to hurt us. We have to stop them."

"Then we'll call the police," Blaine announced. "There's no need to take justice into our own hands. Nothing good will come of that."

"They killed your uncle. I know it!"

Jesse turned to Blaine, desperate to convince him of the truth before April tainted his friend's thoughts. "We didn't hurt the major. I promise you we didn't."

Uncertainty fluttered through Blaine's gaze. "I

don't know what's going on here. What's that on the table?"

"It's your uncle's book," Sienna explained. "We found it. I have a feeling the major thought April's brother was guilty of Benjamin Soldier's death."

"What?" Disbelief stretched through Blaine's voice as he turned to April. "You don't even have a brother."

April's nostrils flared. "They don't know what they're talking about."

"You need to hear us out," Jesse said. "Please."

They waited for Blaine's response, and Jesse prayed things wouldn't continue to escalate.

CHAPTER
FIFTY-ONE

SIENNA WATCHED BLAINE, praying he didn't do anything irrational.

But what a situation he'd walked into.

She would take the gun from April . . . but she feared April would pull the trigger as soon as she saw Sienna move. In a small space like this . . . any sudden actions could be deadly.

They would each need to be very careful right now. But, as a last resort, Sienna *would* make a move. Otherwise, they might all die here in this space.

"April, why don't you put the gun down?" Blaine finally said, trepidation in his tone.

"What?" Her voice climbed in pitch. "I can't do that. These guys are trained. They'll kill us both."

"We don't want to hurt anyone." Sienna kept her voice even, hoping not to trigger any more emotions.

"We're just trying to figure out what happened to your uncle—and three other men from the squadron. Someone is targeting these people, and it needs to be stopped."

"I've also been concerned about what's happening." Blaine's gaze fluttered between each person in the room. "But this still isn't making sense."

"We don't need to talk!" April's voice rose unsteadily. "We need to figure out what to do with these guys before they hurt us."

"April . . ." Blaine turned toward her, his shoulders slumping with seeming despair. "You're scaring me."

"Tell Blaine about your brother, April," Sienna prodded. "He needs to know."

Blaine's eyes widened. "I would know if you had a brother . . . right?"

April's gaze darkened. "I only discovered he existed five years ago."

"That was before we were married." Blaine stiffened. "Wait . . . you purposely kept that information from me. Why?"

"It's hard to explain. But he needed my help. Neither of us had anyone else, only each other to depend on."

"What did you do, April?" Sobering realization filled Blaine's voice.

Moisture filled her gaze. "While Richard was stationed in the Middle East, someone confronted him one night. It was dark outside, and he couldn't see the man's face—only that he was wearing a US military uniform. This guy ordered Richard to tip off the bad guys so they'd know where to find Benjamin. Said if Richard did what he was told, no one else would be hurt. And if he didn't . . . then the whole squadron would die in a mysterious bombing."

"So, Richard told the terrorists looking for Benjamin where he was posted?" Blaine asked.

"He only did it because he was under duress." April's voice climbed again. "They were all going to die. Only afterward did Richard realize he'd been set up. He realized someone powerful had wanted Benjamin dead. But Richard couldn't come forward. If he did, he knew he'd be blamed."

"That still doesn't explain why you're killing men from the squadron," Jesse said.

"Wait . . . you're responsible for those deaths?" Blaine stared at April, a mix of shock and repulsion in his voice.

Tears ran down April's face as they waited for her answer.

Jesse couldn't believe any of this.

Yet here it was.

The truth.

The ugly, ugly truth.

"The major must have remembered something that happened over there." April sniffled. "He began to question each of the squadron members. One of them told Richard what he was doing. Told Richard that he remembered seeing him sneaking out one night. Everything started to close in. Richard could go away for life if the truth came out."

"What?" An airy quality captured Blaine's voice. "Did you kill those men?"

"I was only doing what I had to do. I didn't want to do any of this. I had no choice. Richard is the only person I have left."

"You had me . . . wait." Blaine shook his head. "That's why you married me, isn't it? Not because you love me. But because you wanted to be closer to my uncle and find out more information."

April glanced at Blaine, tears in her gaze. "I honestly did start to love you. I didn't know that would happen when we first met. I really didn't. But I was also desperate to help my brother."

"If the major knew this was a coverup, why didn't he just go to the FBI?" Jesse asked. "Why all of this?"

"I never talked to him about it, but I can only imagine that he was afraid he'd look guilty also," April said. "He did have culpability in Benjamin's death. From what I understand, he was paid off to turn a blind eye—not that he was going to mention *that* in his book."

"What happened to cause him to write this book now of all times?" Jesse's thoughts still raced as he tried to put the pieces together.

"My uncle was diagnosed with pancreatic cancer about six months ago." Blaine swallowed hard. "He didn't want anyone to know. But the doctors gave him less than a year to live."

"He knew if he wanted to tell his truth that it was now or never," Sienna muttered.

"But this still isn't over." April stiffened again. "I've been trying to eliminate any threats. But now I have to figure out what to do with you."

"April . . ." Blaine stared at her, begging her with his gaze to do the right thing.

She shook her head. "I'm sorry. But this is just the way it has to be."

But before she could say anything else, Sienna charged toward April. Grabbed her arm. Slammed it against the wall.

April's gun went flying.

But not before a bullet blasted through the air.

CHAPTER
FIFTY-TWO

JESSE SAW what was happening and sprang into action.

He dove toward April, his shoulders ramming into her legs.

The two of them collided on the floor.

April fought back with a surprising surge of strength as she struggled against his hold.

Jesse needed to subdue her—before she grabbed that gun again.

He grabbed her wrists, trying to hold her in place, to stop her from doing something else she might one day regret.

But Jesse paused when he saw Blaine storming toward them.

Sienna placed a hand on Blaine's chest and

stopped him in his tracks. "April can't continue doing this. We have to stop her."

Blaine opened his mouth to speak but then shut it again. He looked helpless. So helpless.

"You're not going to stop me!" April screeched.

But before April could do anything, men in black jackets flooded into the room.

"FBI! Everyone freeze and put your hands up."

Sienna leaned toward Jesse as he pushed himself up on his elbows. "Are you okay?"

He sat up farther and nodded. "I am now."

Relief rushed through her. "I'm so glad."

He studied her face a moment. "It's almost as if you care. That's . . . touching."

"I do care." It almost pained Sienna for the words to leave her mouth. But they were true. Thinking that Jesse had almost died in front of her had brought all kinds of realizations.

Mostly the realization that she didn't want to lose this man.

Even though Jesse had been brought into her life through less-than-ideal circumstances, he'd quickly found a real place in her heart.

But now he'd need to decide whether he wanted to stay or go.

Sienna obviously couldn't force him to remain in their strained relationship, staying at a ranch in the middle of nowhere while giving up his career with the FBI.

But they'd have time to talk about that later. Right now, they had to deal with the fallout of April and all she'd done.

"Are you guys okay?" Ian tucked his gun back into his holster as he approached them.

Sienna rose and helped Jesse to his feet.

"Now we are." Jesse touched his side and grimaced. "How'd you know to come?"

"We were following some of those leads you gave us," Ian said. "We came here to ask Blaine more questions. That's when we walked into this. We heard April's confession. We know what's going on, and we have agents out looking for Richard so we can talk to him."

"Maybe this is all over. Finally." Jesse slipped his arm around Sienna's waist and leaned into her.

"Let's hope." Ian's gaze flickered back and forth between the two of them. "I'll need you two to stick around. We'll have questions for you."

"Of course," Jesse said.

Ian paused and turned to Jesse. "And, for the

record, I never thought you were guilty of anything people said you were involved with."

"I appreciate that."

"I have a feeling you'll be cleared soon."

Sienna could only hope so.

But, for now, maybe Jesse could enjoy this victory.

CHAPTER
FIFTY-THREE

TWO WEEKS LATER, Jesse settled into his new accommodations at Vanishing Ranch.

He'd never seen himself being content in a bunkhouse in the desert in the summer.

But he felt happier now than he had in a long time.

He'd officially turned in his badge. The FBI had cleared him of any wrongdoing involving his undercover work.

And he'd accepted a job here at the ranch.

It was all quite the life change, but he was ready for it.

A knock sounded, and he turned.

Sienna stood at the door with a grin on her face. "You want to take a walk before it gets too hot outside?"

"With you? I'd love to." He rose from his bed where he'd been slipping on his shoes and met her in the doorway.

Instead of moving outside, they lingered in front of each other a moment.

Finally, Jesse leaned toward Sienna and planted a soft kiss on her lips. It was one of many they'd shared over the last week.

"I'm really getting used to that," Sienna muttered.

He smiled. "I hope so."

He took her hand as they stepped outside into the dry heat of the early morning.

Mornings here were his favorite. Everything just felt so . . . peaceful. Being here almost made him feel like he'd stepped back in time, to an era when things were simpler. There was no traffic. The TV was hardly ever on. Most evenings were spent outside talking to one another or gathered around a bonfire.

"I just talked to Charlie," Sienna started. "April is officially behind bars awaiting trial."

"That's good news, I guess. It's just too bad that four people had to die before that happened."

"At least Stephen and the guard I left with him are safe." The police had found Stephen and the guard both unharmed in a storage facility outside of town. April had stashed them there until she could figure out the best way to stage their accidental deaths.

April had talked her ex-boyfriend into helping with her dirty work. The man was still in love with her and would do whatever she wanted, from the sound of it. Authorities had found him in Tuscan and arrested him.

They'd also brought Richard in. He'd been hiding out in Idaho but had come forward after April's arrest. He'd affirmed what April had told them about Benjamin Soldier.

Richard didn't appear to be responsible for any of the deaths of his squadron members, and he claimed he hadn't known what April was doing.

However, he mentioned that someone else at the top was involved.

The FBI thought he was blowing off steam and trying to deflect from any involvement he may have had.

But Jesse had his doubts. He, Sienna, and Charlie would keep looking into what happened until they knew for sure that everyone involved was behind bars.

It also appeared, based on some correspondence found on the major's computer, that Major Benning was the unnamed source who'd contacted Charlie.

For some reason, he'd changed his mind before the two of them could meet.

Ian had let Jesse read the major's unfinished manuscript.

There was one thing that stuck out in his mind.

The major had written, "The Florida attack wasn't the work of terrorists."

It was the last thing he'd penned in his book.

He'd been referring to the terrorist attack that had triggered Benjamin Soldier to join the army again.

They were also going to look into that.

But, for today, they would decompress.

"We still need to figure out what to do about those marriage papers." Sienna slowed her steps as they walked toward a fence to the east.

"I thought your friend could destroy those records."

"She could," Sienna said. "If I asked her to."

Jesse paused and took both of Sienna's hands into his. "What do you say we don't have them destroyed?"

She raised her eyebrows, not bothering to hide her surprise. "What are you suggesting?"

"I'm suggesting that the two of us give this a shot."

"Marriage?" Airy disbelief captured her voice.

Jesse shrugged. "This relationship. Let's see where it goes."

Her eyebrows climbed higher. "You mean it?"

"Of course, I do."

"But anyone in your shoes—and in their right mind—would want out."

"Maybe I'm not in my right mind." He grinned.

Sienna let out a laugh. "Maybe you're not."

"Don't get me wrong. I know marriage is a big step. A really big step. But I don't feel right walking away from it. To be honest, I don't really want to."

"If I'm being honest, I've kind of liked the idea of being married to you all along. And not just on paper."

He grinned again. "That's what I like to hear."

"I bet it is, cowboy."

"I have something for you." Jesse reached into his pocket and pulled out a jewelry box.

Sienna's breath caught when she saw it. With shaky hands, she reached for it and opened the velvety top. Her eyes widened when she pulled out the jewelry inside.

"It's a necklace with a heart-shaped pendant," she murmured, holding the gold chain to the light of the rising sun.

"I know you feel that after that attack in Munich

everything changed. Maybe you even think it changed for the worse. But I'm here to tell you that all those changes only made you stronger, made you more beautiful. Don't ever let anyone tell you differently."

Tears glimmered in her eyes. "Oh, Jesse . . ."

"I mean it. Whatever happens between us, never feel ashamed of something that was out of your control. You're a survivor. You have every right to be proud of that fact."

Grasping the necklace in her hands, she threw her arms around him and pulled him close.

Jesse gladly obliged.

When she drew back, her arms still remained around his neck as she gazed into his eyes. "I always knew you were special."

He pushed a hair behind her ear. "Did you? Is that why you married me before I had the chance to say no?"

She chuckled. "No, but maybe that should have been my plan. Now, enough talking . . ."

Instead of saying anything else, Jesse leaned toward her. His lips met hers in a long, slow kiss.

None of this had been in Jesse's plans . . . yet he knew he was right where he should be.

~~~

If you enjoyed this book, please consider leaving a review!

Necessary Risk, Hudson's story, is coming soon!

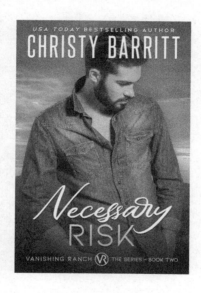

COMPLETE BOOK LIST

Squeaky Clean Mysteries:
   #1 Hazardous Duty
   #2 Suspicious Minds
   #2.5 It Came Upon a Midnight Crime (novella)
   #3 Organized Grime
   #4 Dirty Deeds
   #5 The Scum of All Fears
   #6 To Love, Honor and Perish
   #7 Mucky Streak
   #8 Foul Play
   #9 Broom & Gloom
   #10 Dust and Obey
   #11 Thrill Squeaker
   #11.5 Swept Away (novella)
   #12 Cunning Attractions
   #13 Cold Case: Clean Getaway

#14 Cold Case: Clean Sweep

#15 Cold Case: Clean Break

#16 Cleans to an End

While You Were Sweeping, A Riley Thomas Spinoff

The Sierra Files:

#1 Pounced

#2 Hunted

#3 Pranced

#4 Rattled

The Gabby St. Claire Diaries (a Tween Mystery series):

The Curtain Call Caper

The Disappearing Dog Dilemma

The Bungled Bike Burglaries

The Worst Detective Ever

#1 Ready to Fumble

#2 Reign of Error

#3 Safety in Blunders

#4 Join the Flub

#5 Blooper Freak

#6 Flaw Abiding Citizen

#7 Gaffe Out Loud

#8 Joke and Dagger

#9 Wreck the Halls

#10 Glitch and Famous

Raven Remington

Relentless

Holly Anna Paladin Mysteries:

#1 Random Acts of Murder

#2 Random Acts of Deceit

#2.5 Random Acts of Scrooge

#3 Random Acts of Malice

#4 Random Acts of Greed

#5 Random Acts of Fraud

#6 Random Acts of Outrage

#7 Random Acts of Iniquity

Lantern Beach Mysteries

#1 Hidden Currents

#2 Flood Watch

#3 Storm Surge

#4 Dangerous Waters

#5 Perilous Riptide

#6 Deadly Undertow

Lantern Beach Romantic Suspense

Tides of Deception

Shadow of Intrigue

Storm of Doubt
Winds of Danger
Rains of Remorse
Torrents of Fear

Lantern Beach P.D.

On the Lookout
Attempt to Locate
First Degree Murder
Dead on Arrival
Plan of Action

Lantern Beach Escape

Afterglow (a novelette)

Lantern Beach Blackout

Dark Water
Safe Harbor
Ripple Effect
Rising Tide

Lantern Beach Guardians

Hide and Seek
Shock and Awe
Safe and Sound

Lantern Beach Blackout: The New Recruits

Rocco

Axel

Beckett

Gabe

Lantern Beach Mayday

Run Aground

Dead Reckoning

Tipping Point

Lantern Beach Blackout: Danger Rising

Brandon

Dylan

Maddox

Titus

Lantern Beach Christmas

Silent Night

Crime á la Mode

Dead Man's Float

Milkshake Up

Bomb Pop Threat

Banana Split Personalities

Vanishing Ranch

Forgotten Secrets

Necessary Risk (coming soon)

The Sidekick's Survival Guide
The Art of Eavesdropping
The Perks of Meddling
The Exercise of Interfering
The Practice of Prying
The Skill of Snooping
The Craft of Being Covert

Saltwater Cowboys
Saltwater Cowboy
Breakwater Protector
Cape Corral Keeper
Seagrass Secrets
Driftwood Danger
Unwavering Security

Beach House Mysteries
The Cottage on Ghost Lane
The Inn on Hanging Hill
The House on Dagger Point (coming soon)

School of Hard Rocks Mysteries
The Treble with Murder
Crime Strikes a Chord
Tone Death (coming soon)

Carolina Moon Series

Home Before Dark

Gone By Dark

Wait Until Dark

Light the Dark

Taken By Dark

Suburban Sleuth Mysteries:

Death of the Couch Potato's Wife

Fog Lake Suspense:

Edge of Peril

Margin of Error

Brink of Danger

Line of Duty

Legacy of Lies

Secrets of Shame

Refuge of Redemption

Cape Thomas Series:

Dubiosity

Disillusioned

Distorted

Standalone Romantic Mystery:

The Good Girl

Suspense:

Imperfect

The Wrecking

Sweet Christmas Novella:

Home to Chestnut Grove

Standalone Romantic-Suspense:

Keeping Guard

The Last Target

Race Against Time

Ricochet

Key Witness

Lifeline

High-Stakes Holiday Reunion

Desperate Measures

Hidden Agenda

Mountain Hideaway

Dark Harbor

Shadow of Suspicion

The Baby Assignment

The Cradle Conspiracy

Trained to Defend

Mountain Survival

Dangerous Mountain Rescue

Nonfiction:

Characters in the Kitchen

Changed: True Stories of Finding God through Christian Music (out of print)

The Novel in Me: The Beginner's Guide to Writing and Publishing a Novel (out of print)

ABOUT THE AUTHOR

USA Today has called Christy Barritt's books "scary, funny, passionate, and quirky."

Christy writes both mystery and romantic suspense novels that are clean with underlying messages of faith. Her books have won the Daphne du Maurier Award for Excellence in Suspense and Mystery, have been twice nominated for the Romantic Times Reviewers' Choice Award, and have finaled for both a Carol Award and Foreword Magazine's Book of the Year.

She is married to her Prince Charming, a man who thinks she's hilarious—but only when she's not trying to be. Christy is a self-proclaimed klutz, an avid music lover who's known for spontaneously bursting into song, and a road trip aficionado.

When she's not working or spending time with her family, she enjoys singing, playing the guitar, and exploring small, unsuspecting towns where people have no idea how accident-prone she is.

Find Christy online at:
www.christybarritt.com
www.facebook.com/christybarritt
www.twitter.com/cbarritt

Sign up for Christy's newsletter to get information on all of her latest releases here: **www.christybarritt. com/newsletter-sign-up/**

13311742R00203